I0671422

SLAVER'S DOZEN

A TALE OF KLITZMAN'S ISLE

By

PAUL BLADES

Dark Visions Publications
darkvisionspub@gmail.com

All characters and events portrayed in this work are
fictitious

Other books by Paul Blades:

* Available as a paperback and Kindle at Amazon.com and an ebook at bdsmbooks.com
** Available as a paperback and an ebook at pinkflamingo.com

CHAPTER ONE
TEN GIRLS TAKE A TRIP

In a three story commercial walk up on a small side street in lower Manhattan, a man descends a narrow, dimly lit staircase. When he reaches the street level, he puts down his small valise and takes a set of keys out of his pocket. He drops the keys in a mailbox with the label 'Paradise Productions'. He removes the label and places it in his side jacket pocket. As he opens the door to the street, he looks back up the stairs and smiles. In two hours a cleaning crew will have erased any trace of his presence. He picks up his valise and steps into the street. He will find a cab at the corner. When he gets in he tells the driver, "Kennedy Airport."

* * * * * * * * * * * * * * *

"Mary, Mary, come over here," a nervous middle aged woman's voice said. "Don't get separated from the group."

"Oh, Mom," Mary replied. "Will you please stop fussing. I'm just going for some coffee. Do you want some?"

"No, no, none for me," her mother answered, giving a big sacrificial sigh.

Mary, a raven haired beauty, and her mother were waiting for a plane. They and about another twenty five or so nervous, young and attractive girls, their parents, friends and/or boyfriends. The plane was scheduled to leave at 10:30, but Mr. Paderovski wasn't there yet. It was already 10:15. Nothing could happen without Mr. Paderovski. Mary's mother was in a frazzle.

"Are you sure you want to do this, Mary?" she asked her daughter when she returned with a cup of hot decaf. "It's so far and for so long. I'm going to be worried about you every night."

"Mom, please don't do this," Mary replied, exasperated. "I've made up my mind. I know you love me and you worry, but really, it'll be all right."

The trip had been weeks in the planning, when you considered the long screening process and the many interviews. You see, Mary, and nine other lucky, model quality, young women had been selected to be representatives of Paradise Productions' international tour. All of the girls had stars in their eyes. Lana and Brenda, Brittany and Danielle, Carol, Karen, Kit, Rene, Sheila and Mary were the finalists and winners of a three month's long talent search. They had just the right youth, vitality, innocence and beauty to model the ready to wear fashions of Paradise's many garment industry customers. They were about to launch a new, world wide promotion, with stops in Madrid, Genoa, Athens, Ankara, Bangkok, Manila and more. It was a lifetime opportunity.

A slender, strawberry blonde girl, Kit, bumped into a similarly coiffed, shapely, young girl, Sheila. They turned and looked at each other.

"Oh!" they both cried. "You made it too!"

"Yes, and so did you," answered Kit excitedly. They had met at one of the auditions and had promised each other that they would both make the cut. The two hugged excitedly.

"I just knew that you'd make it!" Sheila said her arms still around her friend.

"Me too!" Kit replied. "I mean, that is, I thought that you would make it too!"

"I know what you mean," Sheila said, excusing the other girl's slip of the tongue.

"Do you think that they'll let us bunk together?" Kit asked.

"Oh, I hope so," said Sheila.

If anyone in the airport waiting area had taken the time to notice, the ten girls chosen for the "Paradise Tour" were all of the same body type, lithe and curvaceous, all of approximately the same size, between 5'6" and 7", all blessed with ample cleavage to best show off the customers' designs. It was simple to explain. If all the girls were approximately the same size, they could exchange clothes easily. They would need only one set of each garment and any of them could wear it on any given day. All the girls were between 20 and 21.

And the selection process had not been limited to just physical beauty. Mr. Paderovski and his assistant, Ms. Bowers, had explained carefully the need for girls who would not embarrass the company. A very rigorous reference system had been in place. They had all had to submit to medical exams to prove their lack of prior 'unacceptable behavior'. Aids, HIV, any other possible medical problems had been ruled out. Mr. Paderovski wanted girls who were 'pure and demure'.

And Mrs. Bowers was there to make sure it stayed that way. All cell phones were banned for the trip, no email, no instant messenger, no text messages. The parents and loved ones had been assured that the girls would return as innocent as they had started out.

Finally, Paderovski appeared. "Ladies, ladies, ladies," he called out. "Please gather round me. There's been a change of plan!"

A groan arose from the assembled group.

"It hasn't been cancelled?" Karen cried out. She was the redhead of the group and a thick mane of curly hair, two shades short of orange, flowed down to her shoulders. She had fine, pale skin, colored like cream. She had mostly grown out of freckles, but a small enough hint of them remained, enough for her to retain a bright sheen of youth. She had known this would happen! Her Irish born mother had warned her in her thick Irish brogue, "Don't get yer hopes up, Karen. That way it won't hurt too much when it falls through." Karen had had enough of her mother's depressing world view. It drove her father to drink and now was driving her out of the house. What a chance to escape! But now it looked like her mother was right. Was she condemned to eternal disappointment, she asked herself.

'No, no," Paderovski answered, "it's not cancelled. No dear. It's just that we've been offered the use of the corporate jet belonging to one of our sponsors. We're going to be traveling in high style!"

A general buzz of excitement went around the assembled group. Even Karen's mother was impressed.

"Does it have a kitchen and movies and stuff like that?" Carol asked. Carol was a chestnut haired brunette. Her hair hung down her back almost to her waist. She was there with her boyfriend, Peter. They had cried and promised to write to each other every day while she was gone. She had given him a list of the hotels they would stay at and their itinerary. "It's just for three months," she had told him tearfully. It surely broke her heart to see him so dismayed. But all in all she thought that it was for the good. They would see if they really loved each other. If their relationship could survive this separation, then she knew that it was real love. Peter had been pestering her to 'do it" with him for almost six months. Well, pestering is maybe too strong a word. Let's just say that he expressed his desires for "physical fulfillment" of their love in a strong, emotional way. Carol was glad that she had held out. She wanted the first time to be with someone she would love forever. When they came back, if their love was still strong, she would be sure.

"Yes, yes, yes," Paderovski answered her. "All the amenities. Now everybody, hand in your tickets. Ms. Bowers, will you assist me?"

Ms. Bowers was a tall, brown haired young woman of about twenty six. Her five years of greater world experience seemed like a hundred to these young girls and they doted on her. She had led them through the auditions, helped them dress, dried their tears. When Mr. Paderovski had told the girls that they had to pose in almost scandalous, tiny bikinis, she had trimmed their pubic hair down to narrow little beards. She helped them screw up their courage to walk out to the photo set and helped them pose against the plain, blue backdrop. The girls all looked up to her. She was virtually model quality herself. Now all the girls crowded around to give her their tickets.

"We have to move over to Gate 21," Paderovski told the girls. "When we reach the boarding area, you can say your goodbyes. I have passes for you all. Only members of the party that are actually flying can go up to the gate."

Paderovski waived a handful of computer printed ducats. He was kind of an odd choice for the director of a promotion company. He was well built, muscular. He had rough features and large, meaty hands. His voice was deep and gravelly. But his tender treatment of the candidates belied his somewhat fierce exterior. He spoke to them gently, almost fatherly. He had personally delivered the good news to each the winners of the competition, calling them in for a special interview in his office. All of the girls were overcome with glee at winning. They were somewhat surprised that the departure date was so soon, a mere three days later. But, this was the world of high fashion where everything was fast.

Paderovski hoisted his valise and waived the crowd on. "Let's get going," he said. "It's a long flight to Madrid."

"But our bags," Brenda said nervously. "Where will we check them in?" Brenda was the nervous type. She had told herself so many times that she was wasting her time trying out for this trip; there were so many other beautiful girls. The night before her final interview, she had chewed through all the nails on her right hand. She prayed that Mr. Paderovski wouldn't notice. He hadn't and here she was. She was one of the five blondes of the group. Her hair was a silky, golden color. She wore it in a pony tail. When Mr. Paderovski had loosened it and draped it over her shoulders for one of the many test shoots, she had almost collapsed in fright. He had reached around her from the front and removed the pony tail holder with his arms over her shoulders. His body had been pressed close to hers. She could smell the strong, masculine scent on him, her breasts, nipples stiff, jammed into his chest. That night she had lain in bed and fantasized about kissing him. She blushed now every time she saw him. She was blushing now as he answered her question.

"We'll take the luggage directly to the plane. A baggage handler will stow it in the freight compartment. Now, come on girls!"

The small crowd flowed towards Gate 21. Many a head turned in the terminal as the ten stunning beauties strolled hurriedly towards their bright futures. They had been all told to dress their best and all the girls were wearing their smartest, sexiest clothes. Although the trip had hardly begun, they had started to think of themselves as models already. They knew that all eyes were on them, and they liked it.

When the group reached the entrance to the loading gates 20 through 27, Paderovski called a halt. "Okay everyone. Say your good byes. Next stop, glamour!"

The girls kissed and hugged their loved ones. All except Rene. She was the odd girl out of the group. First of all, she liked to play with girls. And was she looking forward to this trip! She got wet just looking at the other models. And on the day of the bikini shoot, she had had to run to the bathroom and run cold water over her face. She didn't want to be leaking through her bikini bottom. Rene, in spite of her soft, stylish name, was a hard case. She liked it on top. Her family was all back in Duluth. She had left her lover in their Lower East Side walkup this morning after a night of torrid lovemaking. She could still smell her discharge on her fingers. She watched the skirt of one of the girls, Lana, a light brown skinned, Latina beauty with shoulder length jet black hair, ride up on her well formed thighs as she reached up to hug her mother and father goodbye. Rene felt a tingle in her pussy.

The girls finally started separating as Paderovski urged them on. They waived good bye as they zipped through the metal detector. He hurried them down to the gate. One of those rolling stairs had been brought up and the line of giggling, excited girls descended it. It was windy and they struggled to keep their tiny skirts from blowing up and exposing their panties as they crossed the tarmac. One by one they handed their single bag of luggage to the attendant and climbed the stairs into the jet.

The inside of the jet was as plush and luxurious as they had imagined it would be. Ms. Barlow hustled them to their seats. Paderovski entered last. "Sit down girls! Buckle up!" he shouted to them. When he saw that they were all seated, he went to the door that separated the pilot's cabin from the passenger compartment and knocked on the door twice. The sleek, shiny jet began to inch forwards. The girls all gave off a big cheer.

It took about twenty minutes to get to the edge of the runway; it was a busy day at Kennedy Airport. As the girls heard the jet rev its engines prefatory to its mad dash for the sky, they looked at each other nervously. It was going to happen! It was really going to happen! The pilot released the brake and the jet began its race down the runway. A few moments later, they were in the air.

CHAPTER TWO
THE FRIENDLY SKIES

Ten beautiful, smartly dressed, young women sat in the well cushioned seats of a 360 Starjet hurtling eastwards over the Atlantic Ocean. After the takeoff, there had been a round robin debate on what in flight movie to watch. Three of the girls, Sheila, Carol and Brittany had voted for "Maid in Manhattan" with J-Lo and Ralph Fiennes. Lana, Karen and Brenda opted for Hugh Grant in "Love Actually". Rene, Mary, Danielle and Kit wanted to watch "Brokeback Mountain". It had taken some time, but after Ms. Bowers explained that they probably had time to watch them all, they decided to watch J-lo first, Hugh Grant second and "Brokeback Mountain" last. Rene wanted to throw up.

They were in the middle of "Love Actually" when Mr. Paderovski turned on the cabin lights and announced that they were going to have a toast. The girls were delighted at the prospect of some real champagne. Ms. Bowers had a tray full of elegant champagne glasses all full to the brim with what she described as Dom Perignon. The tray made the rounds until every girl held a long stemmed flute of champagne in her hand. "Now, you've got to drink it all," Mr. Paderovski called out, "or it's bad luck." He looked around to make sure that all the girls had their glasses ready. "Here's to our tour," he called out. "May everyone's dreams come true!" There was a general cheer from the girls and ten flutes of champagne went bottoms up. No one commented on the fact that neither Mr. Paderovski nor Ms. Bowers participated in the toast. When all the glasses were collected, the movie went back on and the girls slumped back into their comfortable seats to enjoy the show.

After about a half an hour, Ms. Bowers got out of her seat and checked up on the girls. They were all sound asleep. Ten blissfully ignorant, beautiful faces slumped in their seats, mouths agape, eyelids fluttering. Paderovski motioned for Ms. Bowers to take her seat and went to the control cabin. He entered without knocking. The pilot, a thirtyish, blond haired lad, with shoulder length hair and a golden handlebar moustache, looked at him and nodded. He picked up the radio transmitter and made a call.

"Any station, any station, this is flight 2733 out of Kennedy, do you read me? Any station, any station, this is flight 2733 out of Kennedy, do you read me? Over."

A heavily accented voice replied in English.

"Flight 2733, this is Lisbon, do you copy? Over."

"Lisbon, this is Flight 2733, I read you loud and clear. I have lost all pressure in my fuel pumps and am losing altitude fast. Do you copy? Over."

"I copy 2733. What is your position? Over."

"I'm about 300 miles, ….oh my God, my engines have cut off, I'm going down, repeat, I'm going down."

The pilot pressed the throttle forward and the plane began to descend rapidly to the black waters below. It was a dark, moonless night, heavily overcast. No running lights of any other planes were in sight. No ships could be seen from horizon to horizon.

"2733, 2733, do you read me, this is Lisbon! Over."

"I'm going down, Lisbon, I can't level her off. I'm going to try and make a water landing. I don't think I have enough control. We're coming in too fast......."

At this point the pilot shut the radio off. The plane had descended from 15,000 feet to about 2500 feet in less than a minute. It would have dropped right off of any radar screen that had been tracking it. Paderovski hustled to the back of the plane. The flight recorder and the GPS transmitter had been removed from the front cabin and stowed and rewired in the luggage compartment. Paderovski pulled a lever and the precious belongings of ten beautiful young women were strewn over the Atlantic along with the flight recorder and the GPS box. The sea beneath the jet had a depth of over 20,000 feet. It was still shallow enough that the signal from the high tech equipment would be ascertainable, but deep enough so that no submersible would be tempted to try and recover them. The plane would be presumed sunk after an emergency landing attempt that crashed open the luggage compartment. The personal belongings that would be recovered would be returned to the grieving families. After several months of investigations and computer modeling, the tragedy would be traced to a possible fault in a $25.00 coupling that linked the fuel tank to the fuel pumping system. A corrective modification would be ordered in all 360 Starjets.

This particular Starjet continued to cruise at 2500 feet for the next three hours. Its new course was south by south east. The jet had been retrofitted with an extra fuel tank to ensure that there was sufficient fuel for their destination since at this low altitude, air resistance was high and fuel economy low. It was just before dawn that the girls began to awaken from the induced slumber. Karen woke first. She couldn't remember watching the end of the movie. She had a slight headache and her mind was fuzzy. She looked around and saw that all the other girls were still fast asleep. Karen had a window seat and she looked out expecting to see miles and miles of clouds and ocean. What she saw was the view from 2500 feet, a different picture indeed! She panicked.

"Oh, oh, oh, we're crashing or something!" she yelled. "Everybody wake up! Oh my God!"

The other girls began to stir. Soon there was a cacophony of excited chatter around the small cabin. Paderovski decided it was time to intervene.

"Ladies! Ladies! Ladies!" he called out in his booming voice. The girls all quieted down and looked to him.

"Now don't be alarmed. We've had some engine trouble, but it's going to be all right."

"Why are we flying so low?" Kit asked, her voice trembling.

"We're flying low to conserve fuel. The pilot had to dump some fuel to gain control of the aircraft. He assures me that we have more than enough left to reach our new destination."

There was a buzz of high pitched feminine voices. "Where's that, Mr. Paderovski?" Mary called out.

"It's a small island just off the coast of Northern Africa. We'll be there in about a half an hour. They've got a large landing strip, fuel and mechanics who can repair the plane. Everything's going to be all right."

"You mean we'll have to get back on this plane after it almost crashed?" Brittany asked. Brittany and Danielle were sisters and the other two of the five blondes.

Brittany was older by thirteen months, but you would never know that they weren't twins. Paderovski had bent the rules a little bit since Brittany was not twenty one, but over twenty two. The sisters were like bookends and had plump, sultry lips, doe like eyes. He would have been an idiot to let them get away.

"No, no, no," Paderovski answered. "I can assure you that none of you will be getting back on this plane. Other arrangements will be made."

The girls all gave a sigh of relief and began to chatter with each other about their close call. Brenda went up to Mr. Paderovski. "May I have my cell phone back? I want to call my mom and let her know I'm all right."

"Why I'm sure that they don't even know about our problem yet, Brenda." He ran his hand through her golden hair. "Calm down," he told her. "Everything's going to be okay."

Not quite satisfied, but too shy to be insistent, Brenda returned to her seat. "What's for breakfast?" Lana called out. All the girls laughed.

Forty five minutes later, the plane set down on a small island located about 35 miles off the coast of West Africa. Unusual for an island of its size, it had a modern jet airport facility. When the jet had taxied to a stop, a rolling ramp was brought up to the door by the ground crew.

"There's a van waiting outside, girls. Everybody get in. It'll take you to where you'll be staying," Paderovski called out to the anxious young women.

"What do you mean, 'where we'll be staying'?" Rene asked. She had looked out the window as they were rolling to a stop and to her this didn't look like any ordinary airport. There was no terminal and lots of black guys were running around in uniforms. And this shit about flying low to save fuel, that didn't seem right either.

Paderovski made a mental note of Rene's truculence. "Everything will be explained in a little while, Rene. Now please don't upset the other girls." Paderovski managed to convey a slight menace in his voice. Rene was taken aback. But she didn't take shit from nobody. She was no schoolgirl.

"I want my cellphone, Mr. Paderovski. I want it now," she demanded. Another of the girls overheard her. It was Carol, the long haired, homespun brunette.

"I'd like to call my boyfriend, Mr. Paderovski, please," Carol asked, not forcefully, but with just a hint of determination in her voice. "I don't want him to hear about our trouble on the radio or something. He'll be worried,"

Paderovski patted Carol on the head. "Don't worry, honey, there'll be phones where you're going, okay? And I doubt that the fact that a small private jet had engine trouble but landed successfully at a small island airport is going to make the six o'clock news. As to you, Rene, the rules apply to everybody. You can wait along with the rest. I'm not going through my bags for everybody's cell phones right now. I've got arrangements to make. This tour is just starting. Don't get yourself known as a troublemaker."

Rene measured Paderovski's response. She wanted this tour desperately. She needed the money. "Okay, Mr. P. I'll play ball." She turned to Carol, a sweet young thing if there ever was one. "Come on, Carol. Let's catch up with the others."

The other girls were already entering the back of a long, black van. There were no seats and so they all had to sit on the floor. "This is ridiculous," Kit complained. She was used to star treatment. She was daddy's little girl. His seven figure income paid for scads of cool clothes and Ipods and video phones and just about everything that she wanted. She wouldn't have been caught dead riding in a black van back home, no windows, no stereo, no seats.

Sheila had attached herself to the stuck up Kit. She had always hung with the cool kids at school and Kit was definitely cool. The other girls, although they were pretty and all that, just didn't have Kit's class. She wanted Kit's class to rub off on her.

"Yeah," she snorted. "This is bullshit. What kind of way is this to run a tour anyway?"

Mary had seen quite a lot of girls like Kit and Sheila in high school and she was sick of them. She had picked them out as the high maintenance type right away. Sure, she was there for the thrill of being part of the fashion world too, but she also had more serious goals. She figured that this would probably be the only chance in her life she would get to see the places they were going to. And for free! And she was going to get paid! Sure, they would be busy and she probably wouldn't get too much tourist time in, but at least she would have gone to these places. And then there was college. She figured with this special 'experience' in her background, it would help her transfer to one of the colleges she didn't get into on the first go round. Princeton maybe, or Barnard. Her board scores had been just a little too low, her grades just a scad short of excellent. But this would put her over the top, she knew it.

"Come on guys," Mary said. "Give Mr. P. a break. I mean, how was he to know that the plane would have trouble. I'm sure this is going to be a setback for the tour. We've got to cooperate."

Karen agreed. She was not, however, in a mood to be quite so polite. "Why don't you guys just stop complaining? We're all in the same boat. There's nothing special about you."

"Please don't fight," Brenda said. She hated conflict. "We'll be okay, Mr. P. said." As far as she was concerned, if Mr. P. said so, it was gospel.

Rene and Carol had just gotten in the van. The back doors swung closed and the van sped away, almost piling the girls on top of one another. The effect of tumbling over each other broke the tension and there was merriment all around. After all, this was an adventure and what could more adventurous than almost crashing?

The girls could not see where the van was taking them. They did not see the high barbed wire topped gate that swung open to let the van speed through. They did not see the modern, one story buildings, the cafes, the dormitories or the lounges, as the van skirted the outer ring of the exclusive resort. They did not see the open garage door, prepared for their entry.

The van was swallowed up and descended to an underground parking area. The two uniformed black men who were sitting in the front seats jumped out of the van as soon as it came to a halt. They rushed to the back and opened the doors. "Everybody out!" one of the men yelled. The other banged his heavy, steel centered baton against the side of the vehicle. Bang! Bang! Bang! The inside of the van resounded with the noise. Even Rene was off put. She and Carol were the first ones out.

"Hurry, hurry, hurry!" one of the guards yelled. A door had opened and another uniformed black man urged them on.

Rene quickened her step with Carol close behind. The girls emptied the van like paratroopers on a low level jump. They hustled to follow Rene and Carol. They had entered a long, brightly lit hallway. There were doors lining it on either side. Their destination was a door at the end of the corridor where yet another black man awaited them. It led to a large room, with a thick red rug and white walls. There was a circular couch in the middle of the room and a number of easy chairs strewn about. The door slammed shut behind them as Sheila and Kit, taking up the rear, rushed in.

"What was that all about?" asked Lana.

* * * * * * * * * * * * *

Back at the plane, Paderovski was taking his time. He had a lot of work coming up and he needed to take the edge off first. He was sitting in one of the comfortable, padded, reclining seats in the Starjet's passenger cabin. Ms. Bowers was on her knees between his legs. Her mouth was energetically working his cock. Her clothes were neatly folded on the floor next to her. On her right buttock, burned deeply into her skin, was a bright red, cursive '*k*'.

CHAPTER THREE
TOUR'S END

The girls had been waiting in the room for over an hour. The door they had entered from was locked on the outside. There was another door on the opposite side of the room, but that was locked too. There was no telephone, no windows.

"What is this shit!" Kit exclaimed. "It's like we were being held prisoner or something!"

Rene didn't like it either. But she wasn't just mad, she was scared. She had a feeling that something was up. There was just no logical explanation for the way they were being treated. Those black guards had looked mean and had treated them like cattle. She looked around the room at her compatriots. They were lounging around the room trying to adjust to the boredom. Carol and Brenda were asleep. Danielle and Brittany were holding hands; they looked scared too.

Karen had taken a strong dislike to Kit and her snobbish ways. She was tired and scared and frustrated. She got up from her chair and confronted Kit, drumming her forefinger into her chest. "Why don't you shut the fuck up!" she told her. "Do you think we want to hear your fucking whining!"

Kit was taken aback by Karen's hostility. But she wasn't going to let that trailer park refugee put her down.

"Don't talk to me like that, trash mouth," she said. "I can say anything I want."

"Listen," Mary said. "This bickering isn't getting us anywhere. Everybody just has to be patient. Someone will…."

At that moment, the door to the room swung open. All of the girls watched, surprised, as three tall, black men, dressed in calf length, black robes stepped into the room. They were carrying frightening looking black batons and large cloth bags that looked like they contained some sort of equipment. A huge mountain of a man, black as coal, with a cruel, hard face followed them in. He was wearing a reddish brown robe. He closed the door behind him and stood there, taking in the vision of youthful, innocent beauty.

Kit, stepping past Karen, ready to assert her superiority, spoke first. "Listen, mister, I want to get to a telephone right away. I want to call my father." Her voice was insolent and demanding. The big black guy smiled and nodded to the other men. The three black robed men advanced as one upon Kit. She shrieked as two of them grabbed her arms and the third ripped her blouse down the front right in two, spilling tiny white buttons throughout the room. She was spun around and the third man yanked the blouse right off of her body.

"Oh, oh, what are you doing? Let go of me!" she yelled. Her arms were held out as leather bracelets were slapped on her wrists. A chain was passed through an eyehook in the ceiling in the center of the room, about ten feet from the door from which the men had emerged.

All of the other girls were on their feet and yelling at the men. Two of the guards stepped forward, putting themselves between the still struggling Kit and the other girls. Karen, put off by the ferocious conduct of the men, stepped backwards, away from them. The third man hoisted Kit's arms above her head and clipped the other end of the chain to her bracelets.

"Stop! What are you doing? Let me down!" Kit yelled, tugging frantically at the chain which now held her arms prisoner. She had been so engaged in protesting her manhandling, that she had forgotten that her pretty, dainty bra was exposed for all to see. "Oh!" she cried out, mortified. "Stop this! You can't do this! Give me back my shirt! Oh! Oh!"

Her assailant pulled a thick, leather gag out of one of the bags and, waiting until she was mid shriek, forced it into her mouth, buckling the belt tightly behind her head. While Kit emitted muffled protests, he took a penknife and cut off her pretty, white, push up bra. Her pale, white globes swung free.

Kit's eyes were as wide as saucers. She kicked out at the man who had gagged her, striking him in the thigh. The man was pushed back as a result of the blow. He laughed and said something to the larger man, obviously their leader. Then he took his baton and touched it to Kit's right breast.

'Crack!' A jolt of electricity passed through Kit's body. She gave out a high pitched, muffled scream. When the man held the baton out to her once more, she tried to pull away. Her eyes pleaded to be spared another taste of the electrified baton. He touched it to her left breast. "Crack!" Kit howled with pain. Her breast seemed to jump as the result of the charge passing through it. "Ohhhhhhhhhhh!" she cried as her body sagged, her weight supported only by the chains that held her wrists. All of the fight was out of her. She looked up forlornly at her assailant, her eyes begging for a surcease of his cruel attack. Seeing her surrender, the man rehooked the baton to his belt and stepped up to the sobbing girl. He reached around her waist and proceeded to pull Kit's bright red, latex miniskirt and the matching thong beneath it to her ankles, all in one motion. He knelt down and unfastened her Gucci sandals tossing them and her skirt and thong over to the side of the room.

While Kit was being rudely stripped, the other girls had all gotten to their feet and had backed away from the threatening guards. None of them had the nerve to come to Kit's aid, especially when they saw and heard the bite of the black man's baton. Danielle and Brittany were holding on to each other. Carol and a few of the others were crying. The rest looked on, aghast. Their minds could not process what their eyes were seeing.

The brown robed man stepped over to Kit and began to admire her naked form. Tears were flowing from Kit's eyes, spoiling her black eyeliner and mascara. The bottom part of her face was covered by a shield of leather. The big man caressed one of Kit's soft, round breasts, tweaking the rigid nipple. Kit tried to pull away, but the man caught the nipple between his strong, fat fingers and drew her back. He smiled at her, bright white teeth offset by a dark, cruel face. He then turned to the other girls.

"My name is Rukimo," he announced in a deep, loud, frightening voice. The girls all fell silent. "I'm going to give you all one chance." He pointed to the floor about ten feet in front of himself. "You will all line up here, hands behind your head. If you fail to obey, you will be punished." The girls all looked at him in shock. "Now!" he added, his voice booming throughout the room.

Crying and shrieking, the girls all obediently advanced to where Rukimo had pointed and lined up, elbow to elbow, their hands clasped tightly behind their heads. When they had all settled into place, Rukimo paused to admire the nine frightened young women. Nine pairs of delicate, long legs, eighteen plump, firm, round breasts, nine beauteous, appealing, fresh, young faces stood before him. Walking to the end of the line, he crossed in front of the terrorized young women like an officer inspecting his troops. He walked slowly, taking in the delightful curves and taut bellies lined up at grotesque attention before him. "Spread you legs!" he called out and the girls dutifully obeyed, parting their delicate, well formed thighs.

The girls watched Rukimo pass by them nervously. Their eyes darted between his huge form and fearsome aspect and the naked form of their tour mate, straining at her chain, tears flowing down her face, her feint whining the only sound in the room.

After the second pass, Rukimo stepped back. He signaled to one of the guards who took a long, rattan cane from one of the bags. He swished it through the air for effect. Kit eyed the man with desperate apprehension. He was going to whip her! "Oh, god," she thought, "please no!"

The guard stepped over to Kit and maneuvered himself into position at her side so that all of the other girls had a clear view of what was to come. A low pitched moan could be heard flowing from Kit's mouth. Tears dripped from her eyes. Her breasts quivered expectantly. She gave out an obscured cry of surprise as she felt the chain above her pulled taut, lifting her feet from the floor.

Another guard knelt at her feet and drew a belt around her ankles. Kit could neither retreat from the anticipated blows, nor flail out with her legs. She could only accept helplessly what the guard was about to mete out.

The guard raised his hand and, not waiting for any further signal, struck the poor girl across the breasts with the hard but supple cane. The sound of the cane striking Kit's soft flesh filled the otherwise silent room. Kit moaned loudly as the kiss of the cane set her breasts afire. As the cane was raised again, she began to plead and beg to be spared. Her voice emerged in the form of a muffled, guttural tongue, the language of some arcane, primitive tribe. As the cane struck her again, this time across her firm, tanned thighs, the unhappy girl screeched in pain. A long, red line formed where the cane had landed, matching the angry red line across her breasts.

Three more times the cane landed on Kit's body, once across her taut belly and again across her pure, white breasts and her tawny thighs. The other girls looked on with horror. None of them had ever seen a whipping and the violence of the scene before them was astoundingly shocking. Mary wondered to herself what kind of hard, cruel world they had entered. She yearned to break her humiliating stance and run for the door. But the door was locked. And where would she go anyway?

Rene watched with the same outraged sense of horror. Her instinct was not to run, but rather to attack. There were nine of them and only four men. Maybe they could overcome them, get one of the batons away from them. She figured that the door the men had come in through, the one opposite the door they had used to enter the room, was unlocked or that the big, heavy man had a key

on him. Her palms were sweaty and her mouth dry from
fear. She could attack, but would the others follow? She
considered her company: the meek, child like sisters
Danielle and Brittany, the soft spoken Carol and Brenda.
Maybe Mary would respond and Karen, the hard, Irish
girl. Sheila was an insecure, in-crowd wanna be. Forget
her. Lana, maybe, but that made only four of them. The
odds were too long. She held her place as the cruel blows
fell on the helpless girl in front of her.

Danielle and Brittany quivered in fear. So swiftly had
their dreams of glamour been turned into a nightmare.
Casting sidelong glances at each other, they fought off the
urge to fall into each other's arms. They had spent a
lifetime together and were linked in their minds like
twins. Neither could remember any significant time apart
from each other. Brittany had even stayed back a year in
school, too devastated by her separation from her sister to
attend kindergarten. "What will these men do to us?" they
thought, virtually in unison.

Both Carol and Brenda cringed as each blow fell upon
Kit. They imagined the cane striking their naked,
displayed flesh. Every lash of the cane against Kit's body
was like a blow to their own.

After the fifth fierce blow from the cane, the black
guard crossed behind Kit. He turned so that he could
strike her back with the cane, wielding it in his strong,
right hand. Five more blows fell from the narrow, supple
cane, each one causing a long line of lacerated flesh on
Kit's back, rump and the back of her thighs. She screamed
and yelled behind her gag as the cane tore into her flesh.
Her body, although confined, had enough movement to
permit her torso to twist and turn in agony. Sweat

descended her body in small rivulets. Her eyes were surrounded by smeared mascara, her once neat and stylish hair matted and in disarray.

Rukimo eyed the young women as they watched Kit's torment end. It had had the intended impact. Nine, quivering, frightened young women stood before him. Nine young women who would meekly follow directions, who would cooperate in their own demise.

Kit was released from the chain and her bracelets joined behind her. A guard pulled the still whimpering girl to the side of the room. She was forced to her knees, her legs splayed apart. A small, silken, black bag was drawn over her head and secured around her neck by a drawstring. One down and nine to go.

Rukimo let the impact of what the girls had witnessed sink in. The message had been clear: they were in the hands of cruel and ruthless men. After a minute of heavy silence, marked only by the feint sounds of Kit's whimpers, he walked to the middle of the room. All eyes were on him. Tension filled the room like a poisoned fog as he thoughtfully perused the nine remaining women. He then pointed to the third girl from the left. "Step over here," he told her, indicating a spot about two feet in front of him. It was Carol, the long haired, shy brunette. She gave a little cry at Rukimo's instruction. She was so frightened that her legs would not obey her. Her body began to shake and she began to sob.

"Come here," Rukimo reiterated in a deep, menacing voice, urging her into action by a single crooked finger. Somehow, Carol found the courage to move and she walked slowly to the designated place before the fearsome black man. She kept her hands joined behind her head, too afraid to move them. Each of the girls pitied her, glad that they had not been the one singled out, but anxious lest they be next. She stood in front of the man, her face a mask of agonized fear. When she had stood before him for several long, anxious moments, Rukimo spoke to her, softly.

"What's your name, pretty one?"

Carol was almost stupefied by the question. She had kept her eyes downcast, too frightened to look this savage stranger in the face. But now she looked into his eyes, seeking, but not finding, a sign of sympathy and kindness there. "C, C, Carol," she stuttered.

"That's nice, Carol," Rukimo replied. He paused a moment, taking in her tremulous form. And then spoke again. "Carol," he said softly, "please remove your clothes."

Carol gave a little whimper at the giant black man's command. She could hardly believe her ears. She looked over at Kit, hooded and bound, her nude form displayed for all to see. Was this her fate, she wondered, her heart beating fiercely in her chest, her breasts rising and falling with each panicked breath. Was she to be whipped like Kit? She knew that she couldn't stand it. She looked back at Rukimo and saw the cold, remorseless visage staring back at her. "P,please," she muttered, her voice barely above a whisper. "P,please don't make me. Please!" Her voice cracked as she spoke.

"Now, Carol," Rukimo intoned, his voice still soft, "you don't want to make me angry, do you?"

"N,no," the terrorized girl whispered back.

"Then please do as I say," Rukimo instructed her. "Take off your clothes now!" The last was said with more than a hint of menace in his voice.

Carol, sobbing, reached to her waist, her hands trembling. She was wearing a plain, white cotton, spaghetti strapped top over a green and black plaid miniskirt. She slowly pulled the hem of her top up, revealing the dainty bra covering her pale orbs. Her pink nipples peeked through the lacy tops, and her breasts swayed invitingly as she struggled to pull the blouse over her head.

When she had removed the shirt, she held it in her hands as if afraid to lose hold of it. She twisted and turned it, tears running down her cheeks. Rukimo motioned to one of the guards who handed him an empty cloth sack. Rukimo held it open and Carol, regretfully, let the shirt fall inside. She hesitated briefly, and then reached behind her back to loosen the strapless bra that held her plump orbs in abeyance. Her breasts trembled and quivered as they were loosened from their bondage. She dropped the bra into Rukimo's sack and crossed her arms over her now bare mounds.

She was mortified that these unknown men would see her private treasures. She had kept herself pure, had denied sight of her tender, soft orbs even to her boyfriend. She knew that men were driven by powerful lusts and that seeing her bare breasts would initiate passions that she had struggled all her not quite yet an adult life to avoid. She knew, too, that forcing her to strip before them was only a prelude to what would be demanded of her. Her stomach churned, her hands were moist with sweat. If only she could stop, could run and hide. But there was nowhere to go, no way to avoid giving these cruel men what they wanted.

Rukimo was pleased at the pleasant, succulent shape of Carol's breasts. Paderovski, as he was known to these ten hapless captives, had not lied. He had delivered a flock of fresh, delightful young females to Klitzman's island. Rukimo yearned to see all of their youthful charms.

"I'm waiting, Carol," he told the cowering young woman. "Off with the skirt!"

Carol closed her eyes and reached behind her to lower the black, nylon zipper that held her skirt firm to her waist. When it had reached its nadir, she slid her thumbs into the waistband and pushed the skirt down over her hips and to the floor. She crouched down to pull the skirt over her black, patent leather shoes, tugging it past the thick, modest heels. As she bent over, her breasts swayed free of her torso, the soft flesh rippling. When she had freed the tiny skirt, she stood up and dropped it into the sack held out before her. She now stood clothed in only her blue and white flowered, cotton, bikini style panties, her ankle length white sox and her black, low heeled shoes.

The long, agonizing process of disrobing created a heavy tension in the room. Standing, waiting their turns, the other girls watched with trepidation. Mary watched with horror. Her throat was dry and heart pounded in her chest. Soon, she knew, she would be standing naked before these men. Her mind raced with thoughts of the implications of the scene before her. They had all been duped. There was no engine trouble, there was no fashion tour. They were now the prisoners of unknown men, thousands of miles away from home. Her arms had begun to ache with the strain of holding them up behind her head. She could feel the sweat running down her face, under her arms, the dampening of the scanty clothes that she, like all the other girls, had been instructed to wear. She had held back her tears, but now she could feel her emotions begin to overwhelm her. She closed her eyes and prayed that what was happening was not real.

Carol did not wait for any further encouragement from the imposing black man before her. She pulled her panties to her feet and dragged them over her shoes. Her long, chestnut colored hair spread around her as she knelt to remove her shoes and socks. When they were off, she hesitated at rising back to her feet. She knew that when she did, the men would see all, that she would be naked and helpless before them. She wanted to stay kneeling forever, to disappear right in front of them, to be whisked away to some other place where she would be safe and freed from fear.

Rukimo reached for one of the black batons carried by the other three men. He poked it under Carol's chin. "Up, up, up," he ordered. "Stand up, pretty girl and let me see you."

Recalling the fierce bite of the baton, the way that it made poor Kit jump and scream, Carol reluctantly obeyed. "Please don't hurt me, mister," she said, her voice a desperate whine. "Please."

"Hands behind your head, girl, and be silent," Rukimo commanded curtly. He was done playing games. "Turn around!"

As she lifted her arms behind her head, Carol turned her back to her tormentor. She could see all of the eyes of her fellow captives glued to her naked frame. She squeezed her eyes shut in shame. Rukimo shoved the black baton between her legs and tapped her thighs. "Spread your legs," he ordered.

Reluctantly, but obediently, Carol moved her thighs apart. She could feel the eyes of the men boring into her back, her pale white rear. She felt her sex exposed, the little lips peeking through her faint, sparse bush. Rukimo stepped past her, closer to the rest of the expectant girls. The three black giants followed suit.

"Strip!" he bellowed. For a moment there was stunned silence as Rukimo's command sunk in. Then, eight frightened young women jumped at his command. In a matter of a minute, blouses, bras, skirts, panties, nylons, socks and shoes were tossed on the floor. Sobs of fear and humiliation filled the room.

Rukimo watched the terrorized girls shed their meager clothing. He had seen their pictures, of course, the ones Paderovski had sent on. But they had been in bathing suits, little ones to be sure, with their sexual parts shrouded. Now they would be revealed in all of their glory.

Having disrobed completely, even down to their pretty, stylish sandals and shoes, the girls all resumed their enforced pose, hands behind their heads, legs apart. Tears filled most of the youthful eyes. The posture they had assumed showed off their fine, unblemished breasts to great advantage, pushing them out invitingly. Their trimmed pubic hair set off their parted labia, forced open by the spread of their legs. Rukimo took another tour of inspection, pausing here and there to caress a luscious breast, or to rub the pussy of a tearful girl. Although the girls had been chosen for their comparative uniformity in physique, naked, all their subtle differences were highlighted. Were breasts like the shells of the ocean, Rukimo opined to himself as he admired the assembled pulchritude, no two exactly alike? Pert nipples, long ones, thick ones, well rounded breasts, thick heavy ones, firm, taut ones that peaked, cone like. Even the areola differed markedly from girl to girl. Some were dark and wide, some pale and small, with almost every variation in between. On Sheila, one of the blondes, he could see the feint hint of blue veins, clouded by the milky whiteness. The Latina girl's breasts were dark, although still lighter than the rest of her skin. A tiny black hair peeked out from her right nipple. Rukimo smiled at the trembling girl as he caught it between his thumb and forefinger. He tugged at it briefly, enjoying the tension on the girl's face and then yanked it out. Lana cried out, more in surprise than pain. She cringed at the intimate contact.

Rukimo paused at the almost mirror like forms of Danielle and Brittany. They were on the far left end of the line. He studied their faces carefully, noting the slight variations, a chin slightly less sharp, eyes a tad wider apart. They both had broad, plump, full lips, accented by the bright red lipstick that they had adorned themselves with the previous day.

"Open your mouth," Rukimo ordered Danielle, who stood next to last in line. She complied meekly. Rukimo pressed two long, thick, black fingers past Danielle's trembling, ruby lips. She moaned as she felt her mouth invaded. She wanted to clamp her teeth down on the insulting digits, to cast them from her mouth. But fear of retribution held her in thrall to the mighty man before her. Her only reaction to the rape of her mouth was to produce two large drops of tears, one for each eye, which trailed slowly down her cheeks, over her chin and down her graceful, soft neck. "Suck," Rukimo commanded in a low, but stern voice. Danielle closed her lips on the man's fingers and, closing her eyes as if to shut out her shame, produced a gentle tugging on them with the suction from her mouth.

With his free hand, Rukimo grabbed one of Danielle's thick, short nipples and twisted it, just enough to cause a hint of what pain could be induced. Danielle whined at the abuse of her flesh, mortified that her intimate parts should be so rudely used before the three black guards who stood behind Rukimo, leering. "Suck it like you mean it, slut," the giant man told her softly. Danielle's mind rebelled at the derogatory label, but her mouth studiously obeyed the command. With alacrity bordering on vigor, she caressed the invasive fingers with her tongue, pulled hard on them, pressed her face forwards and back like she had been taught in the back seat of her boyfriend's car.

"Good, good," Rukimo commented. "And now let's see your sister," he told the despondent girl.

Brittany awaited her turn with trepidation. She had watched the degradation of her sibling from the corner of her eye. Her mind raced with dreadful speculation of what this all meant. The sexual connotations of the act forced on her younger sister did not escape her. She knew that the black man was measuring her, her sister, all of them, for some cruel, unbearable fate and that the act of simulating fellatio on the callous fingers of the big black man was almost certainly a prelude of heinous and foul treatment to come. Rukimo's actions had put paid to any notion that there would be a pleasant ending to this disturbing interlude. Like her sister, Brittany forswore resistance and parted her trembling lips in obedience to Rukimo's command. Giving a little cry, she submitted to the man's outrage. The thick, heavy fingers probed her mouth, depressing her tongue, causing her stomach to heave. Without further instruction, she drew her lips closed over them and caressed them with feigned fervor.

Rukimo maintained his fingers in the young girl's mouth until he was satisfied that she had been sufficiently humiliated. He was tiring of this prolonged psychological torture of this new crop of victims. He pulled his fingers free, wiping Brittany's saliva on her breasts, and ordered the girls to turn around in a loud, harsh voice. They all complied readily. Eight pert little asses presented themselves to his view, eight naked, graceful backs, eight trembling pairs of interlocked hands. Carol was still standing in the center of the room, facing her travel mates. She could feel the menacing presence of the black men behind her. Tears were flowing down her face as she contemplated her obvious fate. She yearned for home, cursed her stupidity in being duped by the illusion of glamour. Her knees trembled with fright.

While Rukimo had conducted his tour of inspection, the tall, black men had gathered the abandoned clothes strewn about the floor and stuffed them into the bag in which Carol had deposited hers. Now, two of the black guards, at Rukimo's signal, carried the sacks containing the leather bracelets and gags to the right side of the line and approached Sheila who was standing on that end. One of the guards pulled her arms behind her and the other clamped two leather bracelets over her wrists. When finished, he clasped them behind her back. Up to now, Sheila had held back her fear and shock. But the sensation of being deprived of the use of her arms, of being rendered unable to mount even the feeblest defense against an assault to her person, broke through her brittle reserve.

"Oh, God, please let us go, please!" she called out. "We haven't done anything, please!"

Ignoring her entreaties, a guard pressed up against her back and, reaching around, one hand grabbing and depressing her jaw, he jammed the business end of a thick, leather gag between her lips. She gave out a muffled moan as it was buckled behind her head.

One by one the young women were bound and gagged. None resisted; all docilely accepted their unknown fate. Only their sobs and whimpers marked their adornment with the instruments of confinement. The third black guard followed in the wake of the other two, fastening thick leather collars around their necks.

When all of the women were reduced to helpless, voiceless victims, they were ordered to turn around once more to face their captors. Kit had been raised to her feet, her hood removed and a collar snapped closed around her neck. A series of short chains were produced and the girls ordered to turn to their right. The frightened but subdued young women were connected to each other, chains leading from the front of their collars to the braceleted hands of the girl before them. Kit was fastened in the front, her eyes darting to and fro in nervous apprehension. The door was opened and nine new, naked and frightened female slaves were led from the room, urged on by the menacing black guards and their fearsome black batons.

CHAPTER FOUR
CAROL MEETS HER NEW OWNER

Carol stood as rigid as a statute, a sense of panic welling up within her, as she watched her friends being led away. She wondered, fearfully, why she had been left behind, singled out, what special, cruel fate was in store for her.

Rukimo had remained in the room. He watched as the last helpless young woman was tugged from the room like a reluctant caboose on the end of a dismal train, a pair of pitiful, despondent eyes peering back at him. Ignoring the wordless plea, he turned to the sole remaining captive. Carol had not yet been gagged and her sobs were quite audible, having reached a new crescendo at the disappearance of her friends.

Rukimo stood before her, his face inches away from hers. His hand descended down her side, over her graceful, naked hip, and down to the fulcrum of her widespread thighs. Carol stiffened as she felt the man seize her sex, something no one had ever done. She felt his thick finger trace a line between her distended nether lips, ending atop her little bud of pleasure. Afraid to even look at her assailant, Carol jammed her eyes closed. As the finger pressed itself into the crevasse of her sex, she felt an unwelcome tingling in her loins.

Carol knew about the pleasures that her honey pot could bring her. She had read the books, heard her friends talk, had even dared to stroke herself, just a little, until a warmth spread from her innocent sex outward and throughout her body. But she had always stopped short of any extended passion. It was wrong to pleasure herself, just as wrong as it would be to have her boyfriend stroke her there. Only holy matrimony and the demands of procreation could excuse or justify the coaxing out of otherwise illicit passions. And now this man, this huge, cruel, callous man had seized her sex and was drawing from her what she had always denied herself.

As the tender cunt began to drip with the evidence of Carol's increasing excitement, Rukimo let his fingers probe deeper into the softening hole. He met a fleshy barrier there, evidence of the girl's sexual innocence. He had known, of course. She had been selected weeks ago based on her medical exam and her almost child like visage. Her face was round, with a tiny, pert nose and narrow, pale lips. Her eyes were deep brown, matching her shiny, long, chestnut hair. They were large and clear, giving her a doe-like appearance. The girl's eyelids trembled as she tried to suppress any sign of the outside world, emphasizing the tender vulnerability that had sealed her individual fate. The others were destined for whatever role in the vast resort their masters chose for them, after suitable training, that is. But Carol's fate was special, and not one to be preferred.

When Carol finally moaned with incipient pleasure, Rukimo smiled and abandoned his invasion of her private place. One of the bags had been left in the room and Rukimo went over to it and removed a slave collar and a four foot long leash. He crept behind the girl and, after lifting and pushing aside the long, silky hair, snapped the collar around her neck. Her body shivered as she felt it clamped shut. Rukimo brought his lips close to Carol's ear and whispered into it, "We're going for a little walk, pretty girl. Keep your hands behind your head and follow me." He attached the leash to the front of the collar and gave it a little tug. Carol pitched forwards and ruefully followed.

She was led out of the same door that her friends had left. There was no sign of them in the corridor. Carol had little opportunity to observe the stark white walls or the plush red rug as she hurried to keep up with the large man's pace. The hallway led to a steel door at which Rukimo pressed a buzzer and waited. A black face peered through a small window, nodded, and Carol heard a heavy bolt drawn open. She was pulled through the doorway and down another hall. At the end, a black guard sat at a large desk bedecked with television monitors. There was an elevator, and when Rukimo caused the door to open, Carol was drawn inside.

Carol could see her reflection in the plain, polished steel walls of the elevator. She flinched at her nakedness, the lasciviousness of her pose. Tears came to her eyes as she felt the elevator lurch upwards. After a short ride, the doors opened and she was dragged out.

What Carol saw stupefied and amazed her. She was led into bright, hot daylight, past a large, black sentry and down a brick walkway. There were low level, whitewashed buildings all around and people, men mostly, walking here and there, dressed in either blue or brown robes similar to Rukimo's. Most astounding of all were the naked women, some at the end of chains like hers, others jogging quickly along the paths, their hands bound behind them, their bodies naked, their mouths hidden behind heavy, leather shields. Were they prisoners like her, Carol wondered. Would she soon be running naked and bound, her mouth hideously gagged, hurrying to god knows what destination?

The men ogled her as they passed by, nodding recognition to her captor. Rukimo strolled purposefully over the narrow walkways, certain of his goal. The young girl blushed with shame as her bare breasts bounced and jiggled, put in motion by the rapid pace. Her hands were glued together behind her head as if cemented there, bound by invisible threads of fear. She had no desire to provoke this cruel giant who led her obscenely displayed body past the staring men and oblivious women. She sensed the cruelty inherent in the man and desired desperately to avoid it.

They finally reached a gated compound. A black robed guard opened the gate and allowed the pair through. The walkway turned to polished, multicolored flagstones and led to a pair of heavy carved wooden doors. As she stood, waiting for the door to open, Carol saw the obscene designs etched into the dark brown wood. Men fucking women, women sucking off men, threesomes, foursomes, women fucking women, and, liberally intermingled with the displays of sexual debauchery, carved images of women being whipped and tortured, their mouths stretched into grimaces of pain. What was beyond this door, Carol wondered fearfully. Was what was displayed a precursor of her own fate? "Oh, god," she pleaded to herself, "please don't let it be true!"

The heavy doors opened and Carol followed her captor's lead inside. The floors of the anteroom were smooth, brightly polished, green and black marble. The walls were a stark white. As she entered the hallway beyond the foyer, Carol observed the large, obscene paintings and prints displayed there. She shivered with fear as she was led down the hall to a teak paneled archway. The archway opened to a large, expansive room, marble floored like the hallway, and bedecked with flowing, lavender pastel curtains along the walls.

Sitting in the middle of the room, centered on a large, overstuffed, pale green couch was the largest man she had ever seen. He had heavy, loose jowls, a broad, flabby chest, thick, round arms and legs. He was dressed in a blood red robe with bright gold threads woven into it, drawn taut across his huge belly, but revealing a thick, hairy chest, matted with the effluvia of his most recent repast. His hair was short and grey, and he had a slovenly face, large, loose lips, a broad, heavy nose. His eyes seemed black, sunk deep into his face. His head was large, an appropriate match for his elephantine frame.

Surrounding the man, and strewn around the room were perhaps a dozen young, beautiful women. They were naked but for short, sheer black skirts that veiled, but hid nothing. One woman lay on either side of the man on the couch, on their backs, their legs splayed wide open, their sexes presented to the man's pleasure. He had a meaty hand on the belly of the one on his left, a large thumb implanted into the woman's cleft. On his right, a large silver tray sat on that woman's belly, filled with small dishes containing sweets and delicacies. The man's left hand was in the process of drawing a succulent morsel to his greedy mouth.

Other than the two women who lay on their backs besides the mammoth man, and two women on their knees between his legs, working their lips and hands over his ample genitalia, the rest of the women knelt in a sort of semi-circle before the man, their heads touching the floor before them, their hands palms up behind their backs. Angry red stripes adorned their proffered back sides and their bare backs. Three black robed guards sporting the ominous black batons stood at attention along the walls.

The mountain of a man spoke. "Ah, Rukimo, a delight to see you," he said. The man's voice was deep and guttural, almost as if his throat was filled with viscous liquid and the words were forced to bubble out. "I see you have brought me a present."

Rukimo brought the naked girl to a halt about three feet from the obese man. She was overwhelmed by what she saw. Never in her life would she have imagined that such a scene could be real. She had read of Arab princes and their harems, oriental despots with their armies of concubines. But she had not considered anything like them to exist in the real world. But here it was, right before her. And she was being presented to him like a newly acquired pet for his approval and delight.

"Yes, Mr. Klitzman," Rukimo replied. "One of the new girls, the one you picked out. The others are being processed as we speak."

"Wonderful, wonderful," the huge man replied. Rukimo, no slouch himself, seemed diminished when compared to this man who he called 'Klitzman'. "Bring her closer," he said. "Let me feel her tits."

Carol gave out a high pitched whine at the thought of this ugly, horrid man, manhandling her precious breasts. The women at his feet parted as she was shoved forwards. "Here, on my lap," the man commanded. His gluttonous eyes shined as he reached out for Carol's body. Rukimo

handed him the leash and he pulled the girl close to him
and then pulled her up on his broad right knee. Carol, her
hands still locked behind her head, started to cry all over
again. Her mind cringed at the thoughts of being ravished
by this ravenous beast. She looked at Rukimo desperately.
"Oh please don't leave me here," she sent to him mentally.
"Please, oh please don't leave me here!"

Rukimo observed the girl's obvious distress. It meant
nothing to him. She was just a thing to be played with, to
be used, and it mattered not a whit to him how or by
whom she was possessed. It was sufficient that his lord,
Klitzman, was pleased.

"I will leave you to your fun, Mr. Klitzman. Nicholai
will be here shortly. He's organizing the disposition of the
plane."

Klitzman had his arm wrapped around Carol's waist,
pulling her up against his soft, fleshy body. "Good, good.
I want to congratulate him. A pretty penny, a pretty
penny."

"As you say, Mr. Klitzman," Rukimo replied. "I'll be
back later." He gave a short bow to his master and
retreated from the room.

Carol was softly sobbing as she anticipated the fat
man's abuse. What had she ever done to deserve this, she
thought abjectly. What sin had she committed?

"Let me see those pretty tits," Klitzman told the
despondent girl as he pulled her torso backwards. Her
breasts lay exposed to his view, the small tender nipples
taut and hard with fear. Klitzman massaged the pair of
soft white orbs with his free hand. He squeezed them like
ripened fruit, measuring their succulence. Carol turned
red with shame at the handling of her breasts. She closed

her eyes and gritted her teeth. She felt the man's large, drooling lips descend onto her left breast and seize her hard nipple, sucking her breast into his mouth. He sucked long and hard, pulling the top third of her breast into his mouth, while his hand pinched and twisted the other nipple, causing Carol to moan with pain. The hand that had encircled her waist, grabbed her hair behind her head and Carol felt her face pulled towards her tormentor's.

A sour, wet mouth covered hers and a stiff, powerful tongue insinuated itself past her tense lips. Carol kept her teeth tightly clamped, dreading the invasion of her oral cavity by the man's foul tongue. The hand on her right breast twisted and turned the nipple harshly, causing Carol to squirm with pain. "Open up!" the man demanded as he increased his torment of the tender breast. Carol cried out in pain and, as her mouth opened to release her exclamation, the man's greasy tongue intruded, filling her mouth, thick drops of drool running over her chin and down to her chest.

As the slimy tongue explored her mouth, pushing aside her tongue, slavering over her teeth and gums, Carol felt the man's hand descend to her taut stomach, sliding down to her loins. She tried to protest, but her words were muffled by the heavy lips that covered her own. The hand pressed into the still moist, tight slit, running roughly against the walls of her crevasse. She felt a thumb and forefinger grab her tender clitoris and squeeze it hard. Pain shot through the girl like electricity. "Ohhhhhhhh!" she moaned into the mouth that covered hers. "Ohhhhhhhhhhhh!"

Carol tried to press her legs together to force out the hand that tormented her. Klitzman just squeezed harder on her clit, tugging and pulling at it while his tongue continued its callous exploration of the girl's abject mouth. "Ohhhhhhhh!" Carol whined. "Please, don't, please, please!" she tried to shout through her captive mouth.

"Open your legs, slut," Klitzman ordered, in an impatient, harsh voice, freeing her mouth from its debasement. "Open your legs or I'll cut out your tongue," he told her.

Meekly, Carol drew her knees apart, praying that the man's torment would stop. He thrust three fingers into her tender cervasse, pressing against the flimsy wall that denoted the girl's sexual innocence. "We're going to get rid of this," the man told her teasingly. "I'm going to pierce it with my prick, but first we've got to get you properly outfitted." He unceremoniously pushed Carol to the floor. She landed on her hip, pain shooting through her. "Kneel there, slut," Klitzman ordered. One of the guards brought over a large wicker basket with several compartments. He drew from it first a thin, round golden collar, with heavy rings on each side. The guard removed the leather collar that had adorned Carol briefly, and substituted the hard, cold, golden collar. One size fit all as there were several holes for a springed tab to fall into, depending on the width of the captive's neck. Carol merited the third hole in.

Once her neck was imprisoned in her gaudy adornment, Golden bracelets were affixed to her wrists and ankles. Carol accepted the confinements on her body resignedly. What was the use of struggle? This man had the mastery of her and there was no prospect of being spared. She knew that she would soon know whether being raped was a fate worse than death.

When she was properly adorned, Klitzman ordered the group of supine women kneeling before him to lock her hands behind her. "Get her ready for a good fucking," he ordered them. "Loosen her up good. And you," he pointed to an obsequious young female at his feet, "suck my cock till it's good and hard."

Carol felt her hands locked behind her. Thick straps were hooked to rings in her ankle bracelets and wound around her thighs, tying them to her calves. Hands spread her knees open, mouths fastened on her breasts. Smooth, knowledgeable hands caressed her. A pretty face appeared before her and opened her mouth with her tongue, gently and soothingly caressing her inner mouth and lips. Carol began to feel her passion rising. She had steeled herself against pleasure when the women had seized hold of her, but gradually surrendered to her rising lust. She felt a mouth engulf her sex, a tongue tracing a hot line between her labial lips. At this, Carol moaned with sexual excitement. She had never felt anything as overwhelmingly pleasurable as the hot mouth that engulfed her moist, lush sex. She moaned again, deeper this time and louder, as the anonymous tongue pressed on her hardened clit, worrying it, enflaming it.

Klitzman watched the seduction of the innocent girl with unrestrained lust. The expert mouth of the slave girl between his legs coaxed his well worn cock into a steel-like hardness. The girl knew not to let her master come, for that would spoil his game and certainly result in one or more painful beatings, or worse. But she was skilled at her trade and could sense just when to release the hot member from her lips and let the obese man's lust subside.

Satisfied that his victim was well enough prepared, Klitzman ordered the slave girls to deliver her to him. The girl between his legs withdrew and he leaned back on the couch pointing his sturdy, thick manhood straight up into the air. Carol felt herself being lifted from the ground by many hands. Hands had circled through her bound arms and over her shoulders. Other hands grabbed her pinioned thighs, her arms. As she was lifted up and presented to the fat man's hard cock, Carol moaned and cried out. "Oh, god, not like this, please, please, don't do this, please!" Her sacred vow to save herself for her marriage bed, to keep sanctified her precious virginity was about to be dashed upon the rock hard meat of this grotesque man. She watched the man's lustful, leering face as she felt the tip of his cock pressed between her throbbing, blood filled lower lips. She moaned again as she felt the lips part and the meat begin to slide inside her.

"No, no, no!" she cried. "Oh, god, no!" Hands pressed her torso down, soft, feminine hands, hands obedient to a cruel and heartless master. The cock began to press upon the thin veil of flesh that barred full entry into her sheath. Suddenly, with one hard jolt, her body was forced down on the sturdy member that had entered her and it tore through the virginal membrane. "Ohhhh!" Carol cried in pain and despair. "Ohhhhh!"

The fat man's eyes rolled back into his head as he luxuriated in the hot, moist warmth of Carol's purse. His hands sought the oozing slits of the women lying next to him, and pressed inwards, delighting in the softness and heat that their proffered pussies provided.

The women who had seized Carol manipulated her torso up and down on Klitzman's unrepentant cock. She felt the hard, thick meat pierce her loins again and again. Hands caressed her breasts, a mouth seized on hers, pressing a hot, firm tongue past her lips. A feminine hand descended down her belly to the nub of pleasure at the apex of her sex and began to caress it, driving her passion to a new height. The pain was gone now and replaced with an overwhelming need for climax. "Oh! Oh! Oh!" Carol cried out as she felt the hot prick rub the length of her sheath, filling her, satisfying a need that she didn't even know that she had had.

Suddenly she felt the cock inside her begin to throb and pulse. Klitzman gave out a mighty moan, shoving his cock upwards, impaling the girl to the depths of her womb. As the hot fluid filled her, Carol felt her moment of crisis peak and, for the first time, felt the electrifying pulses of pleasure that her sex could produce. She came with a loud shout, crying from both humiliation and ecstasy. This evil man had brought her to a height of pleasure she had not known possible and yet he had despoiled her, tore away her innocence, reduced her to a servile sexual slave.

When Klitzman's lust was satisfied, he waved the women away, "Put her on her knees," he instructed them. Carol was placed between the man's open legs. He sat up and grabbed the back of Carol's head by her hair. "Lick me clean, slave," he told her, his voice harsh, the threat behind his words clear. With a sob, Carol placed her mouth over the detumescing prick and wiped it clean with her pursed lips and tongue. She tasted the mixture of Klitzman's spewm, her own musky discharge and the blood from her ravishment. She cried, overwhelmed by the mixtures of feelings that coursed through her. After a few moments, she felt her head pushed back and she was shoved rudely to the floor.

"Good work, cunt," Klitzman told her. "A good start. Now we've got to get you marked." He spat out a command to the guards in their native tongue. A large ottoman was produced and Carol picked up and draped over it on her stomach. Straps bound her there. Her buttocks were prominently displayed. Through her befogged, mind she wondered what the fat man meant by being 'marked'.

"First a taste of the lash, I think," Klitzman ordered. One of the black guards took a long, thin reed from the wall. Carol's mind had cleared at the mention of the lash, and, remembering what Kit had suffered, began to beg and plea to be spared.

"Oh, please don't whip me, please!" she shouted out. "I'll do whatever you want, please, please!"

"You'll do whatever I want regardless, slut. Now take your whipping for my pleasure and your instruction," Klitzman replied. To the guard he said, "Gag the bitch. I've had enough of her caterwauling."

Carol felt a thick, rubber plug installed in her mouth. A thin tube led from it to a small rubber bag. A large black hand began to pump the bag and the plug in her mouth sprang to life. As the air filled it, Carol realized that she would be effectively silenced, no longer able to beg for mercy. "Oh, g...." was all she was able to say, as the plug rapidly expanded to fill her oral cavity. She felt the rubber tube pinched off and a slight hiss as a valve on the front of the plug was shut. "Mmmmmpf!" was the only sound that she could make.

Suddenly a line of fire exploded on her buttocks. She tried to scream, but her voice was silenced. Another and another blow fell across her pale white rear cheeks. She struggled at the bonds that held her to the stool to no avail. Her whole ass was afire, like hot oil had been poured over it. Kit had gotten five blows on her back and rear. Carol expected the guard to stop once he had reached that number, but he did not. Lash after lash descended on her. The pain was unbearable, but had to be borne, as she no longer controlled what sensations her flesh would experience. Klitzman was her master, her lord, her ruler. And when he said to stop, the guards would stop, and not a moment sooner.

What Klitzman was waiting for was for the tool of enslavement to finish heating up. He had had built an electric branding iron. It took less time to heat up and left a cleaner, more precise brand. Rukimo still preferred the old fashioned way of heating a steel rod in a brazier until its tip glowed red. But Klitzman had not the patience for any subtle forms of torture. What he wanted, he wanted now.

When the guard noted that the branding iron was ready, Klitzman signaled the whipping to stop. Carol continued to moan and squirm on the stool, her ass ablaze with the tongues of a hundred flames. She could not see the guard with the branding iron, she did not know that her idea of what pain was was about to be substantially altered. Three of the other slaves moved to hold the girl down, to smother her squirming reactions to her torture.

When she was stilled, the guard pressed forwards. The angry red tip of the iron kissed Carol's flesh. Her body jolted as she felt the first excruciating messages of pain emerge from the surface of her already tender skin. The pain turned into a deep, mind wrenching torment as the rod pushed in on her flesh, on the upper right portion of her right buttock. The black man counted slowly to three, ensuring a deep, clean burn. Carol's screeching echoed through the room, tempered slightly by the rubber plug in her mouth. Mercifully, she fainted.

When Carol came to, she was still draped over the stool. Her ass was on fire. She felt physically drained, as if her physical reaction to the heretofore unimaginable pain had depleted all of her energy. A black satin bag had been placed over her head, and she could hear, but not see, the resumed gluttonous activity of the fat man behind her. She could not see, of course, the angry wound on her rear, or the red tinged salve that had been placed over it. She heard her tormentor bark strange and obscene orders to his slaves, give instructions to the guards, answer a telephone. And then she heard a voice that she recognized.

"Mr. Klitzman, I am happy to see you," the voice said. It was not quite the same as she had previously heard it; the lilt had gone from the voice, also the gentleness and kindness. But there was no mistaking whose it was. Paderovski! "That evil bastard!" she thought, casting aside her demure upbringing, invoking all of the coarse epithets that she could think of.

"Nicholai!" Klitzman answered. "Come in, come in! I must congratulate you on your success. Please, come in."

Nicholai Kodar, thief, murderer and stealer of women entered the room. He saw the proffered ass of the young woman draped over the stool, saw her long brown hair and the angry evidence of her recent branding.

"I see you've met Carol," he said to the smiling, obese man.

"Yes, Carol the cunt," Klitzman replied, "a former virgin."

Nicholai laughed. "You don't waste any time, Mr. Klitzman."

"I never waste time, Nicholai," the fat man responded. "I enjoy every moment of every day, just some more than others. And it was an extreme joy to deflower this fresh piece of ass you have brought me."

Carol heard her ravishment bandied about dismally. "A piece of ass, a cunt, a slut, a bitch, was that what she was, what she was becoming? Her mind protested. "I'm none of those things," she thought, her mind rebelling at the implications of the crude appellations.

"So how's the plane?" Klitzman asked.

"It's going to work like a charm. It's already being repainted and remodeled. A few changes in the wing structure and the nose and no one will ever know that this is the same plane that was reported crashed over the Atlantic Ocean last night," Nicholai answered.

Carol blanched at this bit of information. She had wondered how their flight could have just disappeared, why authorities all over the world were not streaming to the god-forsaken place to save her and her pretty, young friends. Despair washed over her. If they thought that she and the other girls were dead, there would be no rescue, no search, and no reprieve from her dreadful fate.

"A good scheme," Klitzman stated. "My company obtained the plane for virtually nothing as a result of a nice piece of extortion. We'll collect the insurance, $2.5 million, and by next week the refurbished plane will be sold for a million and a quarter. It's a pity we can't get more, but who wants a hot plane?"

"I am pleased to bring us both a healthy profit, Mr. Klitzman."

'Yes, your very considerable share will be on the way to your Cayman Islands account in a few weeks. In the meantime, stay and enjoy our hospitality. Get laid!"

Both men gave out hearty laughs. Get laid indeed.

"And the slave who helped you, she is returned as well?" Klitzman asked.

"Oh, yes, she was quite useful. She is back in retraining I believe."

"Many of the girls do well on the outside and are quite reliable. Most of them have families and loved ones. A simple reminder of what could happen to them is enough to assure loyalty and compliance."

"Well it worked well this time. The girls just fawned over her. And she was an excellent fuck too."

Both men laughed again.

"It is a crowning achievement to bring in ten beautiful young women at the same time as earning us both a pretty penny," Klitzman remarked.

"Well, the plane needed some cover for the flight. As long as we needed our passengers to disappear when the plane did, why not take advantage and bring some delectable whores with us? And it was fun to ensnare them; I enjoyed our charade. It was just a matter of discretion that I limited it to ten. I could have brought fifty. But I brought you a slaver's dozen. You know that one or two always get away."

The fat man laughed. "A slaver's dozen indeed. But fifty," Klitzman mused. "That may be something to work on. A college trip perhaps, the Senior Girl Guides."

"Well, that will be someone else's game," Nicholai said. "With this last payday, I'm retired. Officially."

"Nobody really retires, Nicholai," Klitzman returned. "Once you're in the game, you can never give it up. Too much is never enough."

"An interesting way to put it. We'll see. At least let's call it an extended sabbatical. Okay?"

"Ha, ha, ha," Klitzman laughed, his whole body bounced and jiggled as his mirth was translated to his considerable folds of flesh. "A sabbatical it is. In the mean time, we've reserved a cottage for you and staffed it with some delectable females. Have a good time and we'll talk again when the money clears."

"Thank you, Mr. Kliztman."

"And Nicholai," Klitzman added, "I must repeat, 'a job well done! '"

"Thanks, Mr. Klitzman, thanks." With that, and with one last look at the bound, pretty little Carol, Nicholai, aka Mr. Paderovski, exited her life.

It was time for Klitzman's siesta. He pushed the women who were fawning over him away and struggled to his feet. "Release the new cunt," he told the guards.

Strong hands loosened Carol's bonds. She fell to the floor, too despondent to care what the fat man did to her. Klitzman called out an order in an African dialect and one of the guards brought him a small cage mounted on large rubber wheels. The bag was pulled from Carol's head.

"Get on your knees, cunt," Klitzman ordered harshly. Carol quickly reconsidered her incipient urge to rebellion and pulled herself to her knees. She saw the steel cage, its door open and beckoning to her. Her hands were still bound behind her and her mouth cruelly gagged.

"Get in, slut," Klitzman ordered. "You still have two holes I haven't plowed."

Carol cringed at the obese man's order. It was clear that this gluttonous, callous man could do anything with her. He could torture her, kill her if he wanted. She was dead to her family, dead to the world. She no longer existed except as this cruel man's new toy, his slut. She was reduced to the value of her orifices and the pleasure she could give through her suffering. Her body had been permanently marked. If she could hasten her death, she would. But this man had shown her what real suffering could be. She was sure that she had endured only a fraction of what he was capable of inflicting or having inflicted on his orders. That, she wanted at all costs to avoid. So there was no choice. Obey, and perhaps her suffering could be moderated. Disobey, and find a whole new world of pain.

Despondently, Carol crawled over to the cage. She had to shuffle herself over on her knees. She knew that the fat man was watching her and she rued the swaying and jiggling of her desirable breasts as she moved. If only she could make herself ugly and deformed, she thought.

She poked her head past the cage door and shimmied her way in. The interior of the cage gave her little room to move and she had to kneel with her torso bent over, her knees jammed into her still unmarred breasts. Her long, brown hair splayed across her back like a tattered cloak.

She felt the door closed behind her, jamming up against her naked feet. There was a long leather leash attached to the front of the cage. Klitzman took the leash in hand and turned his massive form to walk to his bedroom. Carol watched his revolting form waddle in front of her. The cage rolled behind him, away from her former world, away from every kindness and warmth she had ever known. Slowly, helplessly, she was drawn deeper and deeper into the depths of Klitzman's hell.

CHAPTER FIVE
KIT'S TURN

The sobbing and crying column of newly enslaved females was led down the long hallway to a steel encased door. A buzzer rang them through, and they entered a long, dimly lit room with cells on both sides. The line of grieving young women stopped in front of the cells. Mary and the other girls looked on with horror at what was certainly to be their new homes for the foreseeable future. Narrow cots sat against the wall in each cell and a thick steel chain hung from the ceiling. A small toilet sat in the corner. There were cells on both sides of the room and the girls could see the cells on the left occupied by naked, hooded women. All of the cells on the right side were empty, as if they had been especially reserved for them, which, of course, they had.

The tall, black guards started from the end of the line. Brittany was first. They unfastened the chain that led to her collar. One of them opened the cell door and guided her inside. The cell was no more than five by ten, just enough room for the cot and a small space next to it. Brittany sobbed as she was separated from her sister. She sobbed as her hands were unfastened from behind her back and fastened to the chain that descended from the ceiling. She sobbed as a hood was lowered over her head.

The hood had tiny ear plugs that emitted a steady hiss of static. The girl would be literally cut off from the world in her cell, neither able to see nor to hear. The chain was tightened so that she was pulled up onto the tips of her toes. After tweaking her delectable breasts, the men stepped from the cell and slammed the door shut.

Danielle and the others had watched as Brittany was confined in her cell. Tears and moans abounded, as the girls saw their own fate. After Danielle and Brenda had been securely fastened, Rene, who was next in line, decided that she would not go docilely. When her wrists were unfastened from behind her, she yanked her arms free and pushed one of the guards out of her way. She ran to the door they had just entered and pulled desperately at the handle. Finding it locked, she cried out frantically from behind her gag, cursing her fate, cursing the guards, cursing the evil man who had enticed her here. The guards laughed as they watched her futile efforts. One of them pulled his baton from his belt and, sticking it between the girl's legs from behind, pulled the trigger. A loud 'crack!' resounded in the room and Rene fell to the floor in agony. The baton was placed against her breast and another 'crack!' echoed from the concrete walls.

Moans of fright came from the other girls still in the coffle line. Unconsciously, they bunched together, seeking protection and comfort in their diminishing numbers. Rene lay almost lifeless on the floor, moaning, curled into a ball. When the baton was laid against her skin once more, she lost all heart and begged with her wide open, frightened eyes for mercy. But slave girls must learn their lessons well. A third jolt from the baton coursed through her. She jerked in pain, moaning and crying. Deciding that she had had enough, a guard grabbed her hair and pulled her to her feet. She was roughly dragged into the next empty cell and her wrists attached to the overhead chain. The insidious hood was installed and Rene was a problem no more. But note had been taken of her tendency to rebellion. She would garner special attention because of it.

The rest of the girls meekly submitted to their confinement. All but Kit, that is. Kit had decided to offer no resistance, but she was surprised when, instead of being placed in a cell, she was taken by the arm and escorted through a door on the far side of the room. She was dragged down another white walled corridor and through another steel encased door. She was pushed into the room and the door slammed shut.

Kit looked back at the door, taken aback that she had been left alone. She looked around her. There was a dais in the middle of the room, raised several feet from the floor. Soft, overstuffed easy chairs sat in a semicircle before the platform. Small spotlights lit the dais and cast a dim glow through the rest of the room. Something special was planned for her, she just knew it. And she knew that that wasn't good.

The girl was alone in the room for at least an hour. At first she sat in one of the chairs and cried. All her life she had been treated with special deference. She had led the 'in crowd' at school. She had had the best clothes, the coolest car, spent her time at the finest resorts and hotels. Servants kowtowed to her, waiters fawned on her. She had set the trends, made the rules. She could make or break anyone's social life with a caustic comment or even a sneer. What was happening was not right.

If only she could speak to her captors, she thought. Her family was rich. Her father would help her. There had to be some way she could convince her captors to allow her to be ransomed. Money had always solved her problems. It had to work the same magic now. Her captors must know who she is, must know that there would be immense profit in returning her to her world. That must be the reason she had been singled out from the other girls, she thought. It had to be.

The naked and bound girl got up from the chair and began to explore the room nervously. It didn't take long to traverse the four strong, silent walls. Her nervousness and fear prevented her from sitting still. She had been whipped in front of all the other girls. She could not understand how she could be treated so meanly.

After about an hour, Kit heard the door to the room opening. The huge black man who had called himself Rukimo entered, followed by two of the giant, fierce looking guards. Kit retreated to the far wall, whining and moaning. All of her resolve to seek exemption from the terrible fate that faced the other girls melted away.

Rukimo stood silently, his eyes boring into the frightened girl's. She knew what he wanted, what he expected. Timidly, she slowly crept across the room until she stood before him. When she looked up at his terrible face, he smiled. "Hello, Kit," he said.

He knew who she was! There was hope! Kit, conscious of her nakedness, mumbled a return greeting through her gag. There was an empty place in her stomach that was churning. Her hands were all sweaty. Unconsciously, she emitted a little whine.

Rukimo put his finger through the ring in the front of the girl's collar and pulled her over to one of the chairs. Sitting in it, he pulled her on to his lap. "It's time we got acquainted, Kit. You have such lovely tits. Do you mind if I play with them?"

Cringing at the outrageous request, Kit shook her head 'no'. What choice did she have really? All of her wanted desperately to protest her treatment, to demand the respect she was due. But, for the first time in her life, she was not calling the shots.

She felt the man's large, rough hand envelope her breast. His hand was cool on her hot skin. He gently probed the soft mound, tapering his caress towards her stiff nipple. He rubbed it with one of his heavy, thick fingers. His ministration sent a tingle to her loins. Rukimo was holding her around her waist with his strong right arm. She could feel his firm grip on her waist. He pulled her closer to him and leaned his head over, taking her left nipple in his mouth.

The warm lips sent a wave of unwanted pleasure through the girl. As the big, black man suckled at her teat, she could see the other black men watching her intently, measuring her. She closed her eyes to shut them out as the insistent lips pulled at her nipple. When Rukimo ran his rough tongue over the areola, she moaned.

Rukimo, having obtained the desired response raised his head. "You're a hot little wench, Kit. I can't wait to fuck you."

At this announcement, Kit's heart fell. He was going to rape her, and probably the other men would too! She would do anything to avoid it, anything. If only she could speak. She looked at the man who possessed her flesh with pleading eyes. She murmured a little prayer to him, tears welling up in her eyes.

"You want to say something, Kit? Is that it?" the man asked her, his voice deep and hard, with just a touch of treacle in it.

Kit nodded. She felt the man's hands reach behind her head and unbuckle the nefarious gag that had stifled her for the last two hours. When the gag was pulled free, it took the frightened girl a moment to find her voice. She was unused to pleading, to deferring to anyone's control over her. She searched for the right words.

"Please sir," she said, her voice cracking, "please don't rape me. I'll do anything else, but please don't fuck me, please. My father has money. He's rich. He'll pay you."

Rukimo feigned surprise. There had been a short debate when Nicholai had sent her pictures and vitals in, as to whether she should be picked as part of the 'team'. Rich fathers could make trouble. But her snooty attractiveness, her plush breasts, her graceful hips and finely sculpted thighs had won the day. Klitzman defied the greatest governments on earth. Why should he defer to a mere American millionaire? But taunting the girl was fun.

"Do tell me, Kit. Is he very rich?" Rukimo asked.

Kit, seeing hope where none had been before, was able to draw out a shadow of her normal confidence, confidence built on wealth and position.

"Oh, yes," she said. "He's very rich. He'll pay you whatever you want. Please let me call him, please!"

That last bit was a little too desperate for Kit's taste, but it was hard to negotiate from strength when you were naked, your hands confined behind your back and you were sitting on the lap of a man who held supreme power over you.

"Oh, I don't know if we can do that, Kit," Rukimo responded. "There are the other girls to think of. If we gave you back, we'd have to return them as well."

Kit thought about the other girls. She couldn't help them really. Her father wouldn't spend millions to ransom other girls, strangers. She decided that the other girls were expendable.

"I won't say a thing. I'll say I missed the plane. You can keep them. Really, I won't say anything." Kit's voice was high and desperate. She looked into her captor's eyes and saw the remorseless lust in them.

"You're such a delicious young thing, Kit. We couldn't part with you after all this trouble." Rukimo answered her, his hand pinching her nipple firmly. "But I'll be sure to tell the other girls that you were willing to betray them. I'm sure that sooner or later they'll get a chance to thank you."

Kit moaned in despair. Beads of sweat were running down her body. Her fear weighed on her like a hundred pounds of bricks. Rukimo moved his hand down to Kit's legs. He rubbed his hand over the length of her thigh as if to emphasize his point. "Such pretty thighs. Do you work out, Kit?"

The question startled the young girl. "W,what?" she asked, timidly.

"You know," Rukimo said. "Do you exercise? Your body is so firm and trim."

It seemed incongruous to the girl to be discussing her private life with this ominous stranger. But, she knew that she lacked the upper hand. Rukimo held all the aces. "Y,yes," she answered. "I try to."

"Oh, and we're very grateful that you do, Kit. It's made your body so desirable." The man's hand moved towards the crux of Kit's thighs. She felt him nudge it between them, prying them apart. She tensed her legs in response and gave out a little "Oh!"

"Don't refuse my hand, Kit," Rukimo said sternly. "I want to feel your cunt. I'll bet it's nice and juicy." The other two men laughed. They had taken seats on the edge of the platform. Kit could see the tenting of their robes, evidence of their arousal. She didn't want them to see her private place. She didn't want to do anything to further enflame their obvious lust.

"Please, don't," she begged, her voice a mere whisper.

"Oh, but I must, Kit," Rukimo replied. "You said you'd do anything, didn't you? I just want to play with your cunt a little. Is that okay?"

Kit bit her lip. She knew what the black man would find. His teasing of her nipple and his oral supplication to her breast had ignited an incipient lust. She was ashamed at her wantonness. "Please don't," she repeated, tears starting to leak from her anguished eyes.

"I insist on your cooperation, Kit," Rukimo said, menace in his voice. He used his hand to push her thighs apart. He let her lean back so that her legs could be splayed widely. "My friends here, Kwambi and Geteye, have been patiently waiting to fuck you. Let's give them a little treat, okay? Unless you want to get started right away?"

"N,no, please, no," Kit protested.

"Okay, then, let's give my friends a little show," Rukimo insisted. He placed his hand on the girl's vagina, draping it with his meaty hand. He was able to encompass it in its entirety and he began to run his palm over the outer lips. "You have a pretty little bush, Kit," he told her. "Do you trim it?"

Kit was distracted by the sensation of the man's hand on her sex. She saw the two black guards leering at her loins. "I, I…" she started.

"Oh, never mind Kit," Rukimo said. "Let's just get this cunt of yours all juiced up, okay?"

Kit moaned in shame and humiliation as she felt Rukimo's finger trace a line between her nether lips. She could feel her loins start to burn with desire. Rukimo placed his finger on Kit's bud of pleasure and rubbed it gently.

"My, my, Kit," he teased her. "You're already wet. I guess all of this talk about fucking has really gotten you hot. Are you sure you don't want to fuck my friends?"

Kit tried once more to bring Rukimo's attention to her possible value to him. "Please, mister, my father will pay you. Please let me go, please don't do this, please!"

She felt Rukimo's finger probe deeper into her glistening slit. "Come on, Kit," he said. "Show my friends your wet cunt." To Kit's shame, Rukimo pried her labia apart, revealing the moist, pink interior of her sex. He said something to the African guards and they laughed.

"You are a wanton whore, Kit," he told her. "I bet I can make you come right here. Want to see?"

The young girl made a move to close her legs, but Rukimo pressed his hand deeper into her sheath. His thumb pressed her clit, twirling it, stroking it. Kit felt her pussy begin to gush. She had let two of her boyfriends fuck her, but had sworn off sex due to the fact that her secretions became a virtual river when she was aroused.

The vast puddle of fluids that she left behind on the bed embarrassed her. Nobody had ever told her about that. Sex was supposed to be neat and fun. She mistrusted the triumph of lust over her mind. And the mess it made!

Now, however, she was leaking her musk over the big man's hand in full view of the two obviously excited guards. Rukimo caressed the walls of her wet, dilated tunnel with his long, fat fingers. Against all her wishes, Kit began to respond to Rukimo's efforts. Her breathing became deeper, her heart started to pound in her chest. She could feel her breasts harden as they filled with blood. As the insistent hand drew her to her climax, her body crossed the line past which she had no choice but to abandon herself to her passion.

The excited girl spread her legs now of her own volition. She tried to press her loins into the hand that was driving her to release. Her hips began to rock. "Ohhhhhh!" she moaned. "No, please stop, please," she begged. But her body belied her stated wishes. When her contractions began, she let out a loud, wild moan. She had never come like this before. "Oh, god! Oh, oh, oh!" she cried out as her pussy pulsed against the fingers that filled her. Rukimo's thumb still tortured her clit, driving her pleasure on and on. "Ohhhhhh!" she yelled. "Ohhhhhh!"

When her passion subsided, Kit experienced an intense wave of shame. She had performed on command for these strange, callous men. Maybe she was a whore, she thought dismally.

"That was good, Kit, very good," Rukimo congratulated her. "You see why we want to fuck you now, don't you? You're a natural whore. And now that we've done something for you, you've got to do something for us."

Kit's face cringed at this announcement. She whined with fear and despair. "Oh, please let me go," she asked. "Please." Her pitiful plea did not mover her captor.

"Have you ever sucked a cock, Kit?" Rukimo asked her.

"Nooooo!" the girl wailed. "Please don't make me do that."

"But, Kit, you said that you'd do anything. I think it's only fair. Now get down on your knees like a good little girl. You'll get the hang of it quickly enough."

Rukimo pushed the girl off of his lap and forced her to her knees. "I think you ought to suck Kwambi off first. Then you can do Geteye and then me. Okay?"

The sullen girl knew that Rukimo was toying with her. She knew that he could make her do anything he wanted. It was clear that they were going to rape her and use her regardless of what she said or did. But to suck a black man's cock! She had never let any of her boyfriends put their dicks anywhere near her mouth. The whole idea disgusted her. But now she was going to do it, do what she had sworn never to do, and to these, these Africans!

Rather than respond to Rukimo's taunts, Kit crawled over to the two seated black men. She knew that she had no choice. Kwambi opened his robe to exhibit his long, thick, hard prick and his heavy, well muscled black thighs. Kit's stomach roiled at the thought of what she was about to do.

"Come, missy," Kwambi encouraged her. "Come suck my cock."

Kit placed herself between the man's knees. Reluctantly, she opened her mouth and took the man's sturdy member in. Nausea swept through her as she absorbed the salty taste of the man's flesh. Having forced her mouth to accept the man's tool, she began to suck on it with all her might.

"Nooooo, missy," Kwambi exclaimed as he pushed her head away. "Not like that, missy. Gentle, smooth." He grabbed her by the hair and pulled her head forwards. "Like your mother's tit, missy, suck it soft, put your lips around it and touch it with your tongue." Rukimo and Geteye laughed.

"Teach her good," Geteye instructed his fellow guard gleefully.

Kwambi pressed Kit's blond head down on his penis. "Now open your mouth, missy," he told her. "Grab it tight with your lips and suck gentle."

Kit pursed her lips around the fat cock. With tears in her eyes, she pulled carefully on the meat with her mouth.

"Now, up and down, missy," Kwambi told her. "Up and down."

The black man had hold of her head and pushed his cock deeply into Kit's mouth. He pulled it up again and repeated the maneuver. "That's right," he told her. "Now you've got it! Oooooo! Yes!" he exclaimed.

Kit meekly allowed the man to guide her in her task with his hands. She could not believe that she was somewhere in Africa, on her knees sucking a black man's cock. Her, Kit Parsons, debutante, socialite, trend setter. She tried to take her mind elsewhere as the steel hard cock pumped in and out of her mouth, scouring itself across her tight lips. But the man's member could not be ignored. Its heat seared her tongue, its hardness and bulk filled her mouth. She could hear the man's moans as his excitement built. She dreaded his inevitable climax, when he would pump his seed into her, his foul bodily fluid. She could feel the cock begin to throb as the man pumped her head faster and faster. She began to whine as she tasted the semi-sweet precum leak from him.

Suddenly, the man's member began to pulse. She heard him cry out just as the first flood of his salty cum jetted against the back of her mouth. "Argggh!" she exclaimed as she fought to withdraw her head from his loins. But his hands held her fast, forcing the cock against the entrance to her throat. She began to gag as the head of the pulsing prick peeked into the entrance to her esophagus. She could feel his wiry pubic hair press against her face, his slimy discharge oozing down her throat. Her mouth was filling with the man's hateful fluid and it burst out over her lips and began to roll down her chin. She felt the man give three last hard thrusts into her mouth and then heard him emit a long, satisfied sigh.

Geteye was next, and he garnered the benefit of Kwambi's lesson to the girl. "You do the work this time, girlie," he told her. Kit, reluctantly obeying, bobbed her head up and down, drawing her tight lips along the length of his sturdy rod. She cried as she pleasured the man's tool, revolted at the act she was so energetically performing. She could not help herself, whining and sobbing as the man pumped his sperm into her mouth. As he came, he placed his hand on the back of her head. "Swallow it, girlie!" he yelled. "Swallow it all!"

When Geteye's passion subsided, Kit turned dutifully to Rukimo. Her face was drenched in tears. She fought back her revulsion as she opened her lips and enveloped Rukimo's hard meat. "Ohhh, Kit," Rukimo moaned as her hot mouth began to ride his cock. "Ohhhh, yes!"

The girl could feel the eyes of the two guards boring into her back as she pleasured Rukimo's prick. This was all a nightmare to her. "This can't be real," she thought to herself. "This can't be really happening!"

But the undeniable presence of Rukimo's merciless prick in her mouth told her that it was real. She had swallowed cum, gallons of it it seemed. And she would swallow more, as soon as this man's passion was driven to its extreme. The room was silent except for the slurping of her mouth as she sought to bring Rukimo to his crisis. Her bound hands twisted behind her as she forced herself to press on.

Rukimo felt his juices begin to rise. "Here it comes, Kit," he told her. "Here comes my sticky, white sperm!" He grabbed her by the top of her head. Just as his cock began to spurt his fluids, he pulled it from Kit's mouth and held her face under his meat.

Jet after jet of his cum splashed onto Kit's face, running over her eyes, down her cheeks. "Ohhhhh!" Kit cried as she felt the thick viscous substance strike her face. Rukimo held her hair fast in his fist.

"Take my cum, whore," he told her. "Take it in your face!"

When he had spurted the last of his load onto the sobbing girl, he released her head and pushed her away. She fell back onto the floor and crawled into a little ball.

"You see why we can't let you go, Kit," he told her as she lay there crying. "You're a natural whore. I knew it as soon as I saw you." He nodded to the other men who stood and walked over to the side of the room. There was the sound of coals being poured onto a grate and the striking of a match. Soon, an acrid odor drifted through the room. Rukimo got to his feet and pulled a small quirt from the belt of his robe. He struck out at the supine girl. The lash smacked hard against her buttocks and she shrieked with pain and surprise.

"Get up, whore," Rukimo told her, his voice heavy and hard. "It's time to make you a slave."

"Ohhhhh no!" Kit exclaimed, suddenly propelled back into life. "Oh God, please let me go, please call my father, he'll pay you, please!"

Rukimo struck the girl again. 'Crack!' The lash ripped across the girl's flesh. "I said get up, cunt!" Rukimo yelled. Kit scrambled to her knees. The remnants of Rukimo's discharge were already drying on her anguished face.

"Please don't make me a slave, please," she whined. "I want to go home, please!"

Rukimo bent over and took up from the floor the gag that had been earlier removed from Kit's mouth. He grabbed her hair at the top of her head and pushed the thick, leather plug against her lips. The girl shook her head in a desperate effort to deny the gag entrance to her mouth. "No, n…." Her exclamation was cut short as the gag was pushed home. Rukimo quickly pressed her head down and buckled it tight. He pulled her head back up.

"You will learn to shut your mouth, whore!" he instructed her sternly. Kit nodded desperately, frantic to avoid another kiss of Rukimo's lash. He dragged her over to where the guards had started the fire. "See that?" Rukimo asked her. "In a little while, the iron that is heating in that fire is going to be pressed against your ass.

It will burn and sear your flesh. You will be nothing more than a branded whore. Property. A slave," he told her. "You will open your whorish legs and mouth to any cock that wants it. You will be beaten again and again to teach you to obey, and for our pleasure." The cruel man allowed the import of his words to sink into the girl's brain. After a brief pause, he told her, "And now I'm going to fuck that sluttish cunt of yours. And you can watch the branding iron get hotter and hotter while I do it."

Rukimo pushed Kit to the floor and retrieved a long, cloth covered stool from the other side of the room. Grabbing the girl by her hair, he raised her up and threw her over it on her stomach. Kit whined and pleaded behind her gag. She had never experienced such callous brutality. The man had gone from a taunting, devilish seducer, to a raging monster in a matter of a minute. She felt her thighs pushed apart. The stool was low and so her ass jutted up higher than her torso. She felt Rukimo's strong hand holding her body in place, as he probed her loins with his resurrected cock, seeking entrance to her womb. She felt the prick's head press past her labia and pierce her moistened slit. "Ugggggh!" she cried from behind her gag in protest and despair as she felt the cock sink deeply within her. Her face was pressed down onto the soft, padded cover of the stool and she shut her eyes to block out the world around her. She could feel Rukimo's sword of flesh rasp against the apex of her sex, stroking the little bud, drawing heat and blood to her loins.

The cock was relentless as it sawed into her, back and forth. It seemed to take forever as Rukimo slowly took his pleasure. Suddenly, she felt a hand in her hair and her head pulled back. "Look, slut," Rukimo ordered her. "See the fire. It's getting hotter and hotter," he told her, his voice harsh and cruel. "Soon the branding iron will glow red and you'll feel its nasty bite."

Kit could not help but watch the glowing embers. At the same time, she could not help the fire growing in her loins. She screamed and cried as the cock ploughed her furrow mercilessly. Her loins grew hotter and hotter; her mind began to fog with the sensation of unwanted pleasure. Like the pulling of a trigger, her orgasm came, sending jolt after jolt through her body. Her whole world centered on the prick that relentlessly agitated her pulsing pussy. When the throbs of ecstasy diminished and her mind began to clear, she could see the fiery plinth before her, the instrument of her torture beginning to glow a bright red.

But Rukimo's cock continued its assault on her womb. Again, she felt her passion rising. Again she felt the tell tale fullness in her loins as she began to climax once more. This time Rukimo came too, pounding hard against the back of the moaning girl's thighs, groaning with exquisite pleasure. His seed filled her hot tunnel and she unconsciously pressed her thighs close against him all the better to receive it. She could feel the pulsing of his muscle within her. She moaned and cried, knowing full well that Rukimo's climax presaged the cruel burning of her flesh.

The mountainous man eased his tool from Kit's sheath. "Are you ready, whore, to be marked as a slave?" he taunted her. As Rukimo stood, the other men began to apply strong, leather straps around her legs and torso. She felt herself being pinioned to the stool. The desperate girl struggled futilely, crying and moaning. She didn't want to be a slave. She didn't want to be burned. She lifted her head up and saw the iron being removed from the fire. Its tip was a bright, searing red. Rukimo had donned thick, leather gloves to protect his hands from the instrument's intense heat. As she watched him circle behind her she tried to utter a piteous plea for mercy, a plea cut off by the efficacy of the gag that filled her mouth.

The giant of a man passed from her sight. The only sound in the room was her own sobbing. She tried to twist and turn her body to frustrate the application of the fiery iron to her flesh. But she had been securely fastened to the stool. Her efforts were of no avail. She could feel the heat of the iron getting closer and closer to her body. She closed her eyes and bit down hard on the leather gag that filled her mouth. As the red hot steel met her tender flesh, she screamed.

CHAPTER SIX
TRAINING

Sheila knelt alone in the large, carpeted training room. Her hands were interlocked behind her head. Her legs were spread wide and her back held straight. She kept her eyes pinned to her reflection in the mirrored door before her. She knew that someone could be watching. The training rooms were lined with ceiling to wall mirrors, but the walls that ran along the hallway outside were made of one way glass. She had seen the other girls being raped and whipped many times as she had been dragged along the hall to her training station for the day. Someone could very well be watching and Sheila wanted, above all else, to avoid another beating.

Actually the term 'day' was somewhat of an anomaly as far as Sheila was concerned. In the dungeons of Klitzman's resort there was no night and day. There was no set schedule; there was no routine to follow. Sheila didn't know how long she had been a prisoner, whether it was day or night, or what her future held. At first, these things had mattered to her. When standing, gagged and hooded in her cell, her legs and arms stretched to extremes, she had tried many methods of counting time. After several minutes, she usually lost count. Her mind would drift from tapping out a steady pace with her fingers or toes to the excruciating pain in her feet, her shoulders and her calves. And the noise, the constant hissing in her ears from the tiny microphones embedded in the hood, she would lose herself in its relentless assault on her mind, actually enter an almost hypnotized state, as it drove out all thought and sensations.

She would try and summon up a mental picture of where she was. She could almost visualize her own naked body hanging at her chains. She had seen the other girls suspended in their cells when she had been returned from her training sessions and she knew that her appearance would be much the same. Sometimes she would wonder whether any of the other girls were watching her as they were dragged back from a merciless beating or a round of brutal use of their bodies.

Alone, kneeling, as the guard who had brought her there had directed, Sheila could not help but review in her mind the cruel regimen to which she had been subjected since that first day when she and the others had cast off their clothing at the command of the big, black man, Rukimo. She had screamed and cried when she had been branded, and had, at first, moaned and wailed as her body had been invaded over and over again by the fierce looking, tall African men. She had cowered and begged for mercy as the whips and canes had driven all thoughts of rebellion or disobedience out of her.

The branding had been the cruelest thing. Even now, the site of her wound still itched and burned as it healed. She could not, of course, see the results of the marking of her own flesh. But she had seen the red, cursive '*k*' on the buttocks of the other girls. She was now somebody's property. But whose? And to what ultimate purpose?

The pretty, social climbing debutante that she had been was gone forever, she knew that. It all seemed so silly to her now: the sucking up to the popular girls, the obsession with the latest expensive fashions, her mania about the appearance of her face, the shapeliness of her breasts. She didn't even know when was the last time she had worn clothes. And the men didn't seem to care whether her face was properly made up, her lips adorned, her hair styled. They practiced their lusts on her without concern for her physical appearance.

The girl was surprised, though, how quickly her mortification and shame at the callous use of her body had faded. The fact that the men seemed able to draw from her unwillingly an intensity of sexual response she had never known had ceased to matter. In fact, she had come to anticipate her use by the strong, merciless, black men with what bordered on desire. Certainly, the extremes of sensation that the steel hard cocks drove her to was better than the unrelenting, oppressive boredom of standing, or lying, bound and hooded in her tiny cell.

Even now, Sheila's expectation that she would soon be used had sparked a growing lust in her loins. She could not but help think of the thick, black cocks that would soon take possession of her. Her parted lips could almost feel the hard meat that would soon slide past them. Strangely, she had come to welcome the presence of a hot, pulsing cock in her mouth. She had discovered a form of power in her ability to coax moans and other expressions of lust from the men who possessed her. She felt a tiny thrill when the salty ejaculations filled her mouth and slid down her throat.

As she knelt, waiting her next round of use, she could see her pleasantly round and firm breasts quiver slightly in her mirrored reflection, as she adjusted her legs and knees to assuage the cramps induced by her long wait. She knew that her taut, firm belly and tender thighs issued a welcome to all who observed her. Her loins waited anxiously for the attention the men would give it. She licked her parted lips nervously.

* * * * * * * * * * * * * *

In the next room, four frightened young women knelt watching, as a naked, black giant administered sharp, painful blows with a rattan cane to the body of a fifth. Brenda, Lana, Mary and Karen knelt in a semi-circle, hands behind their heads, elbows up, as Rene dangled at the end of a chain before them. She wailed and moaned as each blow descended, begging and pleading for surcease.

Rene had paid dearly for her act of rebellion. Each training session began with a slow, steady assault on her body by one or the other of the tall, black trainers. Sometimes, others would follow. Yesterday, or what seemed like yesterday, Mary, the black haired beauty, had taken her turn dancing on her toes as her body was tormented by a long, tasseled whip. As she knelt, unwillingly focused on Rene's torment, she still bore the long, red welts that the whipping had left on her tender, pale, white skin. Lana bore dark purple welts over the light brown skin of her thighs and rear where she had been struck with a riding crop. Karen and Brenda, too, wore evidence of their physical abuse, Brenda especially, as the trainers seemed to enjoy lashing her round, white orbs with the thin, long, bamboo reed.

Rene cried out in anguish as the last, hard blow from the cane struck the rear of her thighs. Tears flowed down her pretty face, covering her cheeks with a sparkling sheen. Each time, she fought the need to cry. Each time, she swore not to beg and plead for mercy. But it seemed that the trainers were conscious of her desperate need to preserve her dignity, to steel herself from the painful, burning sensations of the cane or whip. Each of her tortures had resulted in the breakdown of her reserves, each had ended only when, and sometimes long after, her defenses had been breached, when her whines and moans had become screams and pleas.

Finally, Rene's arms were released from over her head, and she was permitted to fall to her knees before the tall, naked black man. Dutifully, her flesh still burning from her abusive torment, she placed her hands behind her head and leaned forwards to plant a lascivious kiss on the long, thick, stiff tool of her assailant. Today, she would be spared the further humiliation of sucking the steel hard rod to completion. Objegye, today's tormentor, ordered her to kneel at the end of the semi circular line of abject, naked women.

The girls knew the trainer's names. Each time, before their abuse commenced, the men would introduce themselves, as if proud of their roles in the women's degradation. Revealing the names of their tormentors gave the men added power over the women. It was proof positive that these men had nothing to fear. These women would never be able to reveal their identities to any authority capable of bringing their assailants to justice. Later, laying naked and hooded on their cots, or standing, their hands bound above them, their feet arched painfully in efforts to assuage the painful tension on their arms and shoulders, they would recall by name the man who had visited specific acts of abuse upon them. They would see in their mind's eye the gleaming white teeth offset by the dark, black face of their oppressor.

This session, three of the large, black men were with them in the training room. Objegye had wielded the whip. Wanjala and Dume sat naked, stroking their long black cocks, awaiting the completion of Rene's ritual torture.

Objegye circled behind the expectant women. One of them, or more, would now either suffer the anguish of a brutal whipping, or be made to pleasure one or more of the men before the eyes of their fellow slaves. Objegye walked slowly behind the women, enjoying the obvious signs of their tense anticipation. On his second pass, he tapped his cane on Mary's head. "You," was all he said.

Mary scrambled to assume a position in the middle of the semi-circle. Her stomach churned as she worried whether she would take her turn with the dreaded cane, or merely endure the assaults of the men's remorseless and demanding cocks. Objegye motioned the girl to assume a position before him as he sank to the floor and sat before her, legs folded. He leaned back, placing his hands on the floor behind him and gestured her forwards. Mary, obediently, crawled over on all fours and placed her lips on Objegye's prominent tool, her hands on the floor on either side of his hips. Her stomach quivered as the hot, dark meat pressed past her lips, over her tongue and to the very edge of her throat. She had been taught, reluctantly, how to suppress her natural urges and to let the thick, meaty pole push past the entrance and lodge itself within her esophagus. Her gagging reflex was not fully stilled however, and she coughed slightly as her throat closed around the invader.

The routine was well set. First, she would press the rigid pole as deep within herself as she could make it go, until her lips and nose brushed the wiry hair that surrounded the man's cock. Then, slowly, her lips tight against the rigid shaft, her tongue caressing its underside, she would pull her mouth back, letting the cock slide out covered with the wetness of her mouth. She had suffered many strokes of the cane before mastering this technique. Even now, her rear muscles tensed, prepared for the acceptance of a stinging blow should she falter in her task.

The presence of the black man's cock in her mouth and down her throat was the focus of all or her conscious thought. Its unwanted presence and her docile acquiescence in her task shamed her. She had been called whore, slut, cunt and more by the various men who had dominated her since her capture. As she slid her lips back along the long, smooth black skin of Objegye's cock, cupping her tongue to pleasure the fleshy instrument, she felt those appellations justified. They had reduced her to that. What was once a young, vibrant, hopeful woman had been degraded to less even than a common whore. She was a slave, of whom nothing was asked, but from whom all was demanded.

Mary felt the tips of her breasts trace lightly over the legs of the crossed legged man as she wrapped her lips around the bulbous head of his cock. She opened her mouth to draw in much needed air, and, after swirling her tongue over the tip of his shaft, repeated her task, allowing the hot, salty member to fill her.

As she continued her supplications to the African's manhood, Mary felt a presence establish itself behind her. Her legs were splayed widely, as she had been taught, and her pussy's lips were distended, proffered to those that desired entrance. She felt hot thighs press up against hers, a tight, well muscled stomach press against her rear. A hand descended under her stomach, seizing the sensitive flesh that surrounded her pussy's sheath. Fingers, strong, thick fingers, insinuated themselves into her sex's furrow and lightly traced a line along the narrow slit. This was what Mary dreaded most. She hated herself for her inability to prevent the hands and lips of her oppressors from propelling her into unwanted lust and desire. As she pleasured the stiff member of Objegye, she issued a small whine, a tiny, fruitless protest against the stimulation of her sex.

The other girls watched the display of sexual dominance before them as if enraptured. As was required, when Mary had leaned over and taken Objegye's tool in her mouth, they had, in unison, dropped their right hands to their own loins and, spreading their knees as widely as possible, began to manipulate themselves to wetness and passion. Each of them had held Objegye's manhood in their mouths at one time or another, each of them had felt their lusts drawn unwillfully from them by more than one of the callous, determined trainers. Now, they knelt, spectators to Mary's abasement, summoning heat into their loins, feeling their breasts tighten, their nipples harden, as they reacted to their arousal, feeling, and smelling, the musk-like moisture ooze from their enflamed sheaths.

In spite of her efforts to suppress it, Mary's loins began to burn with desire. She could feel her wetness smeared across her pussy lips, feel the thick fingers as they pressed insistently on her clit, thrust themselves deep into her womb. The hand that was tormenting her shifted to her breast, grabbing it firmly, teasing the rock hard nipple. A thick, hard object pressed between her pussy lips. She gasped as she felt the stiff cock slide easily inside her.

Mary had had only two lovers prior to her reduction to sexual servitude. One was a high school boy who she had been dating senior year. They had gone to a party and she had been given some of the punch to drink. It went down easily and smoothly, and it was not until too late that she realized that it had been spiked with vodka. Dizzy, euphoric, she had allowed herself to be led to a bedroom on the third floor of the house. There, in spite of her weak resistance, undermined as it was by her inebriation, she surrendered her virginity. The next morning she had a headache the size of a horse and remorse the size of a house. She never dated the boy again, but saw him smirk every time that she passed him in the halls. For two weeks she prayed that her monthly friend would arrive on schedule. When it did, relief washed over her like a river.

The second boy was someone she met in the small state college that she attended. It was the first semester of her sophomore year, when she met him. They had gone together for several months. Their lovemaking was furtive and uncomfortable. The boy was inexperienced, and the physical act of love had left Mary quite disappointed. She knew what pleasure her little flower was capable of producing, for she often brought herself manually to climax.

Now, her cunt dilated and creamed on command. Thick, black cocks had driven her to explosive orgasms.

Lips, both men's and women's had sent her into virtual delirium. She cursed herself for it, judged herself damned. Even as the throws of her orgasm were upon her, her mind rebelled against the weakness of her flesh.

The girl was still assiduously pleasuring Objegye's cock. The black man moaned, signaling his readiness to discharge his fluids inside her. The rasping of the thick cock against her loins and the hard nubbin of flesh at the vortex of her sex drew a reluctant moan of pleasure from the young girl. Involuntarily, she began to rock her hips against the invader, pushing to meet his thrusts. She did not know, and did not care, which of the other two black men had filled her hot canal with his meat. Her mind had clouded over with passion, all efforts to resist the mesmerizing effects of the stimulation of her loins were abandoned.

Objegye felt his cock begin to throb and, grabbing Mary by the back of her head, pushed her mouth hard down on his cock. Mary felt the member begin to quake and prepared to accept Objegye's discharge. Her loins were growing hotter and hotter as the cock that filled her slit enflamed her. She heard Objegye moan again and felt the iron hard meat in her throat begin to spasm. Her ears filled with the sound of Objegye's pleasure as his jism was pumped down her throat. Her lungs strained at the need for fresh air, but she held her place, allowing the African to take his pleasure within her. The cock within her cunt continued to plow her relentlessly and Mary felt her passion growing larger and larger within her. When Objegye released her head, allowing her to suck in much needed air, her own orgasm began, sending bolts of sharp, hard edged pleasure through her. She moaned and cried as her climax overwhelmed her. She subsumed Objegye's cock within her mouth to draw every drop of his hot cum from him as she rammed back at the insistent cock behind her. Just as her own orgasm began to subside, she felt the need of the man behind her crescendo and the splash of his hot cum within her womb.

Feeling the spasms of the man's cock against the walls of her sheath, Mary's crisis was triggered anew. Her cunt clamped tightly on the hot tube of flesh within her at each exquisite contraction of her inner muscles. She cried and moaned, her voice muffled by the presence of Objegye's softening cock within her mouth. Finally, mercifully, it was over. Mary's heart beat rapidly in her chest, sweat poured off of her body as she felt the two spent cocks withdrawn from her. A slight kick on her thigh signaled her order to resume her place in the arc of panting, lustful women who had witnessed her intense climax. She looked up. It had been Wanjala, an almost lanky man, but with well muscled chest and arms, who had fucked her. He smiled at her in satisfaction.

Meanwhile, Dume had approached the line of women. Like the others, he was naked, and his rampant cock was displayed before him like a heathen totem. He passed behind them, as Objegye had done before him. He had a broad, boney head and wore a thick black beard. His eyes were hard and cruel. He reached out his large, powerful right hand and tapped Karen on her head. The red headed girl jumped with fright. She quickly removed herself from the arc of women and awaited Dume's pleasure, kneeling in the center. She whined with dismay as he signaled her to her feet, his hands holding the end of the steel chain that had so cruelly held Rene a short while before. Her knees weakened and her stomach turned as her wrists were clasped to the chain. She closed her eyes, readying her body to receive Dume's blows. She heard a whistling in the air, the sound of a cane moving rapidly to its target, igniting a line of fire across her soft, tender breasts.

* * * * * * * * * * * * *

While Sheila expectantly pondered the nature of her next training session, and the other girls absorbed their lessons, Brittany and Danielle were lying gagged and hooded, bound hand and foot, awaiting the pleasure of their new owner. Rukimo had immediately assessed their value and their training had been kept separate and apart from that of their friends. He had posted their pictures and some video of their training on the Internet, available only to what was classified as 'Platinum' club members. The response had been gratifying.

After their branding, the sisters were not returned to the regular holding cells. They were taken to a special training room several doors down the hall from the main ones. Once dragged there, they were placed in tiny steel cages, naked and gagged, with their wrists confined behind their backs. The cages faced each other, and the girls could see each other's forlorn faces through the bars. Hours passed, slow, agonizing hours, with the searing pain of their brands still burning them, their joints aching from their confinement. And terror. Nothing in their lives had prepared them for the callous, cruel treatment they had suffered. They had been torn from their safe, civilized lives and thrust into a world of horror. Even now, tightly confined in their little prisons, searching each other's desperate eyes for a single ray of hope, they trembled at what fate their future had in store for them.

The room was brightly lit and did not hide the various instruments of torture and confinement strewn about it. The unhappy young women had no doubt that they would soon learn first hand what torments those medieval instruments could deliver. They had both been coarsely handled and roundly fucked prior to and after their branding. The experience of their carnal abuse left them in no doubt that the use to which their bodies would be put was no longer under their control. As they gazed into each other's eyes, their anxiety for the future gnawed at their very psyches.

The girls were used to each other's comfort, each other's counsel. Now, separated by only a few feet, their eyes meeting in piteous, frightened stares, they might as well have been separated by miles. Neither of them had ever felt so alone. Though they yearned for each other's comfort, they had no choice but to await the designs of their captors.

When the door finally opened, their eyes shifted to the black robed figures who strode in. Their cages sat perpendicular to the door and they could both clearly see the tall, muscular black men as they entered. Something terrible was going to happen, they both knew it.

Two guards had entered, and they were followed by a familiar figure, her hands bound behind her, her mouth gagged. She was tugged along by a short chain that led to her leather collar. It was the woman known to the girls as Ms. Bowers.

Slave girls who were used for the organization's sinister purposes outside of the confines of the resort, or one of the many satellite facilities around the world, were required to undergo a mandatory period of retraining when they returned. Of course, they did not need to be taught their slave mantras, the responses to the standard commands, their sexual techniques. But their resignation to their status as abjectly servile chattel needed to be reinforced. It would not due for them to begin to think of themselves as persons in any real sense. And so the woman who had been permitted for a while, as long as it served her masters' purposes, to respond to the name 'Ms. Bowers', was being reintroduced to the duties and obligations of slavery. Since she had already been trained, she could, it was thought, play a helpful role in the breaking and training of two newly captured girls.

After her wrists were unbound, and her gag removed, the woman took a position on her knees while the men stripped themselves of their robes. They seemed to have a short debate about where to begin. They decided that Danielle who would go first. One of the men, a tall, lean man with an angry, scarred face, unlocked the front of her cage and, grabbing the girl by her hair, pulled her free. The other man, shorter, more muscular, with ritualistic tattoos across his chest and arms, lowered a chain from the ceiling.

When the man removed her gag, Danielle began to plead and whine as she realized what was in store for her. She had reconciled herself to being raped, but she had hoped and prayed that she would not be whipped again. She realized that her prayers had been in vain as her wrists were unbound from behind her back and fastened over her head to the dangling chain.

The girls' cages had been set about fifteen feet apart. There was just enough room in the middle for a slave girl to be whipped. Brittany's eyes teared as she saw her sister prepared for physical abuse. When she heard the tell tale whistle of the whip, she close her eyes. She could blot out the sight of her sister's torment, but not the sound.

It was the tall, lean man who was beating her and he was using a four foot long, thin, rattan cane. The first blow struck Danielle across her naked back. 'Crack!' The sound pierced the room like a shot from a pistol. Danielle's body stiffened and she emitted a high pitched scream. There was just enough purchase for her feet to allow her to spin her body around, to try and dodge the blows. The next blow caught her across her breasts. 'Crack!' Danielle moaned in pain. It was like a vicious claw had been dragged across her tender, plump orbs. She yanked and tugged at the chain in a desperate, but futile, attempt to remove her body from the whip's zone of influence.

'Crack!' The next blow landed across the back of her thighs, the tender skin sending a torrent of fiery pain throughout the wailing girl. Why were they whipping her, she thought desperately. She would do anything they asked. She would debase herself, grovel abjectly before them, spread her legs to open herself to their assaults. Why were they tormenting her, she thought. "Oh, god, why?"

While his partner delivered blow after blow to the defenseless form of the beautiful girl, the other black man kept his eyes pinned to the supine form of Brittany, bound and imprisoned cruelly in her cage. The girl had tried not to look, had tried to shut out her sister's agony, but she could not help but stare as Danielle twisted and turned, performing a kind of *danse macabre* before her. She looked over and saw the other black man watching her, measuring her for what purpose she could only guess. Brittany's stomach turned over at the thought. She began to sob.

Danielle's wretched cries filled the room. Long red stripes covered her body. Her face was tear-streaked, her voice becoming hoarse. Her thighs, her stomach, her buttocks, her breasts were relentlessly assaulted. When the rain of blows ceased, she hung, exhausted and defeated, her arms extended above her, her legs limp.

The men detached Danielle from the chain and led her back to her cage. She cried in relief that her ordeal was over, no matter how brief the respite. Regagged, stuffed and cramped in her tiny jail, her wrists bound behind her, she looked across the room at her sister, knowing that her turn was next.

But when Brittany was removed from her steel cage, she was not lifted to her feet. She was not connected to the chain. She was raised to her knees and forced to spread her pale white, slender, delicate thighs. One of the men, the one who had been staring at her during Danielle's torture, knelt down behind her. She could feel the heat of his chest as he leaned against her back, his breath on her neck. Her bound hands behind her grazed his stiffened cock. Wordlessly, he reached around the girl's torso with both of his hands and placed them on her chalk white breasts.

As she felt the large, hot hands encompass her tender globes, Brittany realized what was being done to her. The thick, strong fingers fastened on her tightening nipples and stroked them delicately. Brittany whimpered as she felt the beginnings of lust in her loins. "Not before my sister!" she begged silently. "Please no!" she thought. The girl felt the hot lips of her assailant press against her throat as the large, skilled hands massaged her breasts.

Danielle looked upon the jet black hands gently caressing her sister's ample, meaty breasts with, if not shock, at least some bitterness. She saw the unmistakable signs of pleasure in Brittany's eyes. Why was she whipped and not her, she protested to herself. The unfairness of it all crushed her. She moaned in despair.

The black man's left hand slowly descended down Brittany's tight, smooth belly. It reached the valley between her thighs and delicately parted the tender lips of her sex. The man found the girl's slit to be moistened, and he drew a small moan from her as he dragged his thick fingers along the edge of the crevasse. Brittany felt her breasts growing hot and tight as her loins began to burn. The man's hands roamed across her body at will, stroking her energized skin, drifting gently down the length of her widespread thighs, while his lips enflamed her neck and shoulders. She could see Danielle staring at her accusingly, as if Brittany had any choice in the designs of her assailant. "Please, please," Brittany begged her sister with her mist filled eyes. "Please forgive me."

Brittany felt her need growing. The man's hand covered her mons and gripped the lips of her sex. Pain mixed with pleasure as he squeezed them tightly. The other hand fiercely twisted a nipple, causing Brittany to let out a muffled moan of pain. But the painful torment was just momentary, enough to highlight the slow, burning pleasure that was threatening to overwhelm her. When the man's finger found her stiff bud atop the apex of her nether lips, Brittany sighed and moaned. She closed her eyes and let her body drift to its unavoidable climax. Her pussy was wet and dilated, and the man was able to plunge his fingers deep within her. He began to rub them rapidly across her hardened clit and her breathing became deep and labored. The girl could not prevent small cries of pleasure to escape and her muffled voice, crying "Oh! Oh! Oh!" filled the otherwise silent room.

The man pulled Brittany's body closely against him as he sensed her crisis approaching. He grabbed her breast with his free hand and squeezed it tightly. His incessant torment of Brittany's tender bud and the lips that surrounded her gushing cunt drove the girl closer and closer to her unwanted climax. When it struck her, her body tensed, much like Danielle's had before her when the supple but hard cane had first kissed her skin. But it was a hard jolt of pure pleasure that coursed through Brittany. Her body spasmed and jerked as her pussy clamped down hard at the jet black fingers within her. "Ohhhhh-hhhhhhh!" she cried, her voice made almost mute by the thick wad of leather imprisoned in her mouth. She nearly swooned in ecstasy.

She was grateful when the hand ceased its torment of her throbbing hole. She gave a little cry as she felt herself pushed over, her forehead to the floor. She felt her thighs spread behind her, her rump lifted up. A hand parted her soft, plush cunt lips and she felt the probe of a rock hard, thick prick. She groaned as she felt it slide easily inside her, reawakening her unwanted passion.

Slowly, and with deliberation, the African rasped his thick, hard meat across Brittany's tender love bud. She began to moan loudly as wave after wave of pleasure passed through her. Danielle looked on with a mixture of horror and awe. What kind of men were these that they could draw such paroxysms of pleasure from her sister, she thought. As she saw Brittany tremble and groan under the tender torment of the black man's hot piece, she was struck with more than a tinge of envy.

The African pulled Brittany's head back by her hair as she neared yet another round of explosive contractions. To her dismay, she saw the bewildered eyes of her sister, her companion, her childhood friend, staring back at her. She gave a throaty moan of shame as the hot prick drove her closer and closer to orgasm. Her bound hands twisted and turned behind her. She yearned to expel the remorseless prick that sawed at her sex. She yearned to fend off the explosive satisfaction of her compelled need. As she moaned with pleasure, she saw herself lost, reduced to no more than a wanton slut. She moaned and yelled out behind her gag as her climax overtook her, sending fierce spasms of pleasure through her body.

When the African had satisfied his own need, discharging his hot cum deep into Brittany's moist and tender womb, calling out undecipherable exclamations in his native tongue, the other black man approached to take his due from the exhausted young woman. While his companion retired from the field of play, he grabbed Brittany by the hair and turned her so that she presented her pale white flanks to her sister. He pulled her to her knees, kicking her thighs widely apart. He released the straps that bound the gag tightly in Brittany's mouth, casting it aside. Standing before her, his long, thick cock rampant, he made his wants clear to Brittany as he pressed it against her plush lips.

Brittany looked up as the man pushed his erect cock past her lips and into her mouth. This was the man with the whip. He had beaten Danielle mercilessly, and without cause. What more might he do to her should she fail to satisfy him, she thought, anxiously. She and Danielle had traded stories of their back seat struggles with boys over the years. She had never acclimated herself to the task of bringing oral pleasure to her beaus. Her stomach had revolted at the hot salty taste of their meat, and the thought of swallowing their slimy discharge was repellent to her. But now she would do it. She would do anything that these cruel men demanded.

With a forlorn whine, Brittany wrapped her lips around the shaft of her assailant. The thick, hot cock filled her mouth and pressed against her throat. She realized that the pace and rhythm of her service to the black man's thick, hard shaft was not to be left to her own devices as she felt the man grab a handful of her thick, blonde hair and push her head down against his stomach so that her nose was buried in his coarse, black pubic hairs.

The tip of the man's cock pressed past the entrance to her throat and descended inside. Brittany began to cough and gag as she was overwhelmed by the man's physical presence inside her esophagus. Her bound hands twisted in frustrated agony behind her. She tried to resist the man's callous efforts, but to no avail. As she bucked and struggled, the man's steel like rod remained lodged in the tight confines of her throat. When she thought that she might suffocate, she felt her head pulled back so that the thick bulb of flesh at the head of the man's instrument passed outside of her lips, allowing her to take a desperately needed gulp of air. She had barely time to suck in the precious oxygen when her head was pressed down again.

Danielle was mesmerized by the tableau before her, watching her sister's degradation. She had often sucked off her boyfriends, and had come to enjoy drawing the groans and shouts from them as she pleasured them and accepted their creamy discharges. But she had never been throat fucked. She watched as the man's prick produced a bulge in her sister's throat as it pressed downwards. She watched her sister's fruitless efforts at resistance, her tears flowing in rivulets down her face. Danielle knew that she would, in the near future, certainly learn to how to swallow a cock so completely, just as she knew that Brittany would inevitably face her own turn at the wrong end of a whip.

The man's deep, guttural groans signaled the inception of his orgasm. As his hot cocked throbbed, jetting pulse after pulse of his salty spewm into Brittany's throat, he withdrew his meat from her mouth, and aimed the tip of his cock at the center of her face. Stream after stream of his cum splashed against Brittany's nose and eyes. She could feel it dripping down, like the thick yolk of an egg. She whimpered and cried at this latest act of humiliating disdain. She felt degraded, reduced to a mere receptacle of this hard and cruel man's lust.

The tall African released Brittany's hair. He picked up her discarded gag and stuffed it back into her down turned, forlorn mouth. He buckled it tightly against her head and dragged her back to her cage. Opening the door at the end, he forced her back in, her breasts squashed against her knees, her face pushed up against the thin steel bars. He locked the cage's door behind her. Wordlessly, the two men readorned their sweaty and muscular bodies with their jet black robes and left the room.

Just as Danielle could still feel the burning sensations of her turn at the whip, Brittany's mind focused on the drying and crusting cum splattered over her face. "This can't be happening!" she thought to herself, woefully. "This can't be real!"

For the longest time, Brittany and Danielle knelt in silent misery, ensconced in their small, steel homes. The former Ms. Bowers knelt silently, her hands resting on her knees, palms upwards, her thighs spread, her gaze fixed at some imaginary point ahead of her. The girls watched her, learning by observation the steel hard discipline required of a slave. At some unseen signal, the woman moved over to Danielle's cage and unlocked it. Silently, she urged her from her cage. In the corner of the room was a toilet and the woman permitted Danielle to use it. When she was done, the woman wiped her and turned on a shower mounted on the wall.

It was necessary to remove Danielle's gag in order to giver her a thorough washing. Danielle stared fearfully at the naked woman as she felt the gag pulled free. Her jaw sore, her mouth dry, she was relieved at this temporary reprieve. She managed a hoarse whisper. "Please, help me," she whined softly. Her eyes were damp with tears, her face furrowed.

'Crack!' The woman gave Danielle a mighty slap across the face. Danielle recoiled in pain. She began to bawl. The woman grabbed her hair and pulled her under the tepid water. Wordlessly, she began to lather soap on the girl's trembling body. Danielle, shocked to silence, resignedly accepted the freedom with which this woman handled her most intimate parts. She stood meekly as her hair was washed and rinsed.

The shower was over quickly, and the woman began toweling Danielle's body down. She dragged a brush through her blond, shoulder length hair, pulling out the knots, causing Danielle to give tiny, half-suppressed yelps. When finished, the woman pulled Danielle back to her cage, her hands still locked behind her, forcing her to her knees before it. Rather than compelling Danielle to return inside her small, steel prison, she knelt before the younger, frightened girl. Her eyes met Danielle's and looked upon her with what appeared to be affection. She stroked the young girl's still wet hair and circled her hand under her chin. Danielle, seeing that the woman had softened towards her, tried to speak, but the woman placed her fingers over Danielle's mouth and uttered a soft, "shhhhhhh." Danielle's lips were trembling with confusion and fear. Moments ago, the woman she knew as Ms. Bowers was callously handling her, enforcing a cruel discipline. And now she was leaning over, her hands holding either side of the young captive's face. Danielle felt the soft warmth of the woman's lips meet hers. She felt her hands run softly over her breasts and thighs.

Danielle was taken aback at the brazenness of the woman's caresses. The woman began to plant gentle kisses over her neck and shoulders. Holding one arm behind Danielle's back, and placing the other between her outstretched thighs, she kissed the nipple of her breast, sucking on it firmly, yet gently, drawing a moan from the young girl. Danielle had never been intimate with a woman. Her hugs and kisses of her older sister had been just that, sisterly. When she had felt strange, warm feeling in her loins, she had broken off their caresses, her physical feelings suppressed by a thousand years of taboos.

But this woman was not her sister. Her fingers probed Danielle's loins, finding them moist and her nether lips beginning to engorge. When Danielle looked over the woman's shoulder and, just as Ms. Bowers found the hard, little nubbin atop her sex, she saw her sister's face, her mouth and chin obscured by her cruel gag, her body cramped and squeezed by her tiny cell. She knew that she should struggle and fight off these strange, Sapphic caresses. She knew that she was displaying the most shameful lust before her own sister. But all thoughts of resistance or struggle were washed away when the woman returned her hot lips to her own, parting them with her insistent tongue. Danielle moaned with passion as she felt her lust rise within her. The woman's hand was expertly teasing her soft, moist pussy. The young girl was surrendering to the demands of Ms. Bowers' lips, her own unrestrainable lust.

But just as Danielle started to feel her heart pumping wildly, just as she began to rock her hips to press her hot cunt against the older woman's hand, Ms. Bowers withdrew. Danielle was gasping with passion, but the woman merely pressed her lips lightly on hers. She picked up the heavy, leather gag that had formerly graced the panting girl's mouth and pressed it against her lips. Danielle gave out a whine of frustration and self pity as the thick leather plug was reintroduced to her mouth and the straps buckled again behind her head. Ms. Bowers rose and guided Danielle back to the entrance to her little cage. She opened the gate and urged the young girl back in. Tears ran down Danielle's face as she considered her shameful display of lust. And yet she yearned for completion, to drink of the older woman's tender lips, to feel her mouth sucking gently on her breasts.

Brittany was next. She knew well enough to remain quiet. Her loins burned with expectancy as Ms. Bowers' hands caressed her flesh, washing away the evidence of abuse from her body. Brittany yearned for the woman's embrace. When she was knelt before her cage, in full view of her sister, who watched ruefully from her tiny prison, she welcomed Ms. Bowers' tongue with her own. She spread her legs willingly, yearning for the delicate touch of her hand. But she too was doomed to frustration. When Ms. Bowers sensed her approaching climax, she ceased her excitation of Brittany's loins and the discouraged girl was regagged and returned to her cage. Ms. Bowers, or the slave who had once been permitted the use of that name, reassumed her position, kneeling silently and still, awaiting the return of the masters.

And so it went. Each time the men returned, one of the two young girls suffered painful and cruel abuse while the other was forced to unwanted pleasure while the men mercilessly plowed her apertures. Danielle screamed and moaned when her rear passage was forced. Brittany, left to dangle upside down, her legs spread, still burning from the whipping of the insides of her tender thighs and the cruel strokes that landed on her sex, moaned and cried while Danielle received lessons on how to accept a long, hard cock inside her throat.

And in between the beatings and rapes, during the lulls in their abuse, the near twins took lessons in lesbian love from their former chaperone. They arched their backs in lustful abandon as the woman caressed their plush cunts with her lips, starting and stopping, keeping them on the edge of bliss, but never letting them topple over it. Gradually, they were coaxed to return the beautiful woman's caresses, running their tongues between her plump cunt lips, taking her stiff, engorged nipples in their mouths.

They had no way to count the days that passed, the countless tense, anxious hours stuffed inside their steel cages, dreading the reopening of the door to their cell. They had lost count of the number of times the men had returned, sometimes only one, sometimes three or four, but more often just two, when, to their surprise, they were both removed from their cages at the same time. They were forced to kneel before their cages, their gags were removed, their wrists unfastened. Five, large, black men had entered the room and they stood around expectantly. The girls were no more than a foot apart, the first time they had been permitted even near contact for as long as they had been imprisoned.

The men waited silently. The girls' bodies trembled as they tried to anticipate their trainers' demands. But, looking upon each other's naked beauty, seeing the hardness of the nipples on each other's pretty, plump breasts, they suddenly knew what was expected, what the purpose of Ms. Bowers' training had been.

It was Brittany who moved forwards first. She crept on her knees to her sister and placed her hands on her breasts. She held them tenderly, squeezing them ever so gently. When she leaned over to place her lips on her sister's mouth, Danielle was ready. A wave of bliss passed through them as their hot tongues intermingled. Their blood boiled as they seized each other's loins. Feeding hungrily at each other's lips, they rolled to the floor. They pressed their lustful bodies together, crushing their breasts, pushing their hot, moist cunts against each other's.

It was Danielle who broke the embrace to run her hot lips down Brittany's taut belly. Brittany responded by circling around so that she could press her mouth against Danielle's glistening slit. The girls moaned with delight as they rubbed each other's stiff buds with their tongues. With Danielle on top, the impassioned women drove each other to a crescendo of lust. It was Brittany who came first, her cries of ecstatic pleasure muffled by Danielle's sex. Danielle followed rapidly, groaning her delight, pressing her face deeper and deeper into her sister's loins.

When the young women's bodies collapsed, their orgasms expended, they were separated once more and forced to serve the lusts of their masters. Plowed fore and aft, each of their orifices plundered by the remorseless cocks of their oppressors, they cried out again and again as they were pushed past the crest of their wild passion.

After the men had left, the girls knelt, reinstalled in their tiny prisons, their mouths once more stifled by the thick, coarse leather of their gags. They stared across at each other, each recalling the caresses they had given and received with such wild abandon, each yearning to enjoy the other's flesh once more.

The rapes and beatings continued. The lustfully obsessed girls were given to understand that they had to earn their sessions of physical love together and they strained to satisfy their oppressor's lusts so they could once again enjoy each other's lips.

Finally, after a ritual cleaning and tantalizing caresses from Ms. Bowers, their sister slave, instead of removing them from their little cages, the men who entered the room affixed wheels to the corners and, after draping the cages with black cloths, rolled them from the room. They were taken down the corridor and into another room. They could hear the entertained voices of men as their cages were rolled to a stop. A man's voice called for silence. Suddenly, the black cloths that had covered their cages were whipped away. There was a moment's pause and the room erupted in applause.

They were on a small, rug covered stage surrounded by cantilevered seats. Harsh lights shined down on them so that they could hear the voices but not see the faces of the men around them. Another cheer arose as they were removed from their cages. When their gags were removed, their wrists unbound, they knelt, their knees inches apart from each others. Although they were surrounded by unknown men, displayed naked on the stage, they could not hide the lust in their eyes. At a signal from one of the African guards, they fell into each other's arms.

There were jeers and catcalls as they fused their bodies into a lustful embrace. When they joined their lips and loins together, the men's voices rose in intensity, their own lusts inflamed by display of lesbian love. When the young sisters climaxed, their sounds of orgasmic bliss unmistakable, the men applauded and cheered.

After the women had achieved completion, they were drawn apart and brought to their feet. Their naked bodies, still evidencing the signs of their recent passionate embrace, were paraded around the stage for the benefit of the crowd. When they were returned to their cages, the bidding started.

Later, lying hooded and bound, the girls had no clue as to the identity of the man who had bought them. They knew that they had been sold and that their bodies belonged to someone who would have god-like powers over them. They would be together; that was all that mattered now. Soon, they knew, their bodies would be delivered to their master, and they would be taken away, far from their homes, their friends, their families, far from any hope of redemption, to some unknown, cruel fate.

CHAPTER SEVEN
ORIENTATION

Now that the girls had learned obedience and to open themselves willingly, even enthusiastically, to their masters, they needed to be made ready to serve the guests and supervisors of the resort. Kit, Sheila, Karen, Mary, Lana and Rene found themselves finally liberated from the underground training area. They had been taken from their cells and chained together in a coffle, hands bound behind them, their mouths securely gagged, and led from Rukimo's dungeon out to the open air of the resort. They were crowded into and then out of the tiny elevator that led to the guest areas and then marched along the brick walkway. As they shuffled along, they looked on with amazement at the many white stone buildings, the blue and red robed men who passed them on their march. But they were truly taken aback at the sight of the verisimilitude of young, naked women jogging quickly and purposely along the path, or serving in the crowded outdoor cafes along the way. They had had no idea that they were part of such a grand enterprise. If they had harbored any hope that their predicament was temporary, it was dashed by the scale of what they saw.

Kit led the parade, and she cringed as the eyes of the passing men ogled her naked form with undisguised lust. The purpose of their training now was perfectly clear. They were doomed to serve as abject whores in this strange dystopia. She was being towed along by her collar, a chain from it leading to the tall, black robed African who had taken charge of them. She clamped her teeth down fiercely on the thick, leather plug in her mouth. Her stomach churned as she contemplated a series of endless days of rapes and beatings at the whim of the merry looking men walking along alone or in small groups, some leading bound and gagged slave girls behind them.

The other girls could barely contain their wonderment. They gawked at the surreal surroundings, stumbling from time to time as their fascination with what they saw overcame their ability to keep a steady pace in the coffle. Mary squeezed tears from her eyes as she realized that the abasement and abuse she had suffered at the hands of the black giants was a mere prelude to her future life. Only Sheila was nonplussed by what they saw. She had discovered a raw lust inside her that yearned for satisfaction. As each man passed, she imagined his steel hard cock plunging deep into her sheath, the heat of his meat in her mouth. Something had broken in her and the creature that had emerged yearned for continuous sexual fulfillment.

The women were led to a small building, not unlike the one from which they had emerged. Two black robed guards stood outside of it, armed with the dreaded batons. A large, steel door was opened for them and they were led inside. There was an elevator, similar to the one they had arisen from the training dungeon in. They waited as they heard its mechanism rumbling, signaling its slow rise from below.

When the door opened, it was crammed with naked, bound women. They were gagged and they had colored tags around their necks. All of them were beautiful and shapely. They were shod in sharp red high heels. Without ceremony, they pressed out of the elevator and streamed out the door that the girls had just entered. Their bodies brushed against each other and the girls' as they desperately sought exit. Their heels clip clopped on the stone tile floor as they forced their way out. Unbeknownst to the new slaves, they had carefully timed schedules to meet. To be late for their assignments would risk a fierce discipline.

After the bevy of frantic beauties had left, the girls were urged into the elevator. It descended slowly. When it stopped and the door opened, they were hustled out. Another small crowd of bound and gagged women was grouped outside the elevator waiting to go up. The coffle of girls was led past them.

A steel door sat at the center of the wall opposite the elevator. The guard who was escorting them swiped a card through a security device and then entered a code of numbers on a key pad. Each card was keyed to a specific code number. This way, if anyone got the key alone, it would be useless. Also, if someone were able to discover the code number of one of the guards, it would be of no avail unless they had the card as well. And the final security precaution was a visual observation of a guard inside the door through a wide angled camera. The camera had the ability to scan the entire vestibule outside the elevator.

The door opened with a loud grinding and a deep thump as solid steel bolts were slid out of their lodging places in the wall. When the door opened, the girls entered a small hallway. At the end was another steel door operated by yet another guard on the other side. It was the guard who was stationed inside the hallway who swiped his card this time. The card he used was recoded daily, tying in the identity number of the guard and a new code number for the keypad. The same procedure was used for slaves on their way out. No woman exited the Slave Center without being bound and gagged and wearing a color coded tag around her neck denoting her destination.

The girls entered a large room with a semi-circular wall opposite them. In the middle of the wall was a small stage on which two women were in the midst of a passionate embrace. Numerous other women were strewn around on the floor kneeling in stiff backed positions, the hands upturned on their thighs. The stage was sunken about ten feet below the level of the floor. The women were kneeling on ledges that descended to the level of the stage. The effect was like a small amphitheatre.

Projected onto the semicircular wall behind and to the right and left of the stage, were videos of women either engaged in various sexual acts with men and other women, or suffering the torment of a whip, or some other torturous device. The girls watched the shifting tableaus with wide eyed amazement. There was no sound from the videos, but they were more than life-sized and the shrieks and pleas of the tortured women in them begging for the abatement of pain could easily be discerned.

The girls were led to the left of the stage where a doorway led into a long hall which followed the semi-circular path of the wall behind the stage. The wall opposite was made of glass and the girls could see into the rooms as they passed. The first room, on their left, was an infirmary, a necessity in a place where women were daily subjected to all forms of physical abuse. The next room, and larger by far than the infirmary, was a huge dormitory. There was row after row of cot-like beds lined up ten across. Each bed was bolted to the floor and had confinements at each corner. Several women could be seen sleeping, large, black eye masks on their faces, bound hand and foot to the cot. The girls were to learn that the lights never went out in any of the slave areas, including the dorm. Therefore, in order to sleep, the women's eyes needed to be shaded. This served well to increase the sense of isolation of the slave, locked into a solitary world of darkness while, ironically, in the midst of a room full of other slaves.

There were no dressers or footlockers. Slaves owned no property. All that was needed by way of hygiene or bodily decoration could be obtained in the large common bathroom.

After being hustled past the dormitory, the girls made another left down a long hallway. They shuffled past, on their left, what was obviously a training room. Several clusters of slave girls were distributed around the room, each learning to master a particular skill important to their new roles. Here the girls would learn the proper way to bathe a man, how to use their pussy muscles to great effect, several different oral techniques and the etiquette of waiting on tables, among other things. Since slaves were never permitted to touch their own bodies in other than incidental ways, except when necessity demanded it, the women were taught the rudimentary techniques of bathing and applying makeup and hair styling on others.

On their right was a large room divided into private cubicles. This was the dormitory for the senior slave staff:

women who had edged past their peak of beauty, but who were useful in training and supervising the younger slave girls. They were afforded some privacy as befitted their status. They also had the right to bring slave girls back to their rooms and demand their sexual services. From time to time, the supervisory staff would be reshuffled, with some being shipped off to the outside brothels and new supervisors moving in. They also served those guests of the resort whose sensibilities and tastes demanded an older, more sophisticated sexual partner.

At the end of the hallway was the administrative center of the Slave Center. Here naked women worked keeping track of the use of comestibles in the cafeteria, the exercise regimen and dietary program of particular slaves. The computer kept track of slave assignments, slaves who were off duty and slaves incapacitated for one reason or another. In spite of being considered as little more than bovine chattel, it was recognized that even a slave needed some time occasionally to rest and recuperate, that they needed something to look forward to. This was accomplished by a seven day on, one day off schedule. The schedule not written in stone, however, and the demands of the guests came first. If for some reason a girl was demanded on what would be her day off, it was unfortunate for her. If there was an unusual influx of guests, or a large contingent of slaves who were physically unavailable for one reason or another, days off were cancelled and all available slaves were drafted for service. Even the service slaves took their turns 'upstairs' achieving only a brief respite from exploitation through the use of their administrative skills.

Once inside the administrative area, the girls were led through a doorway to the left. This area belonged to the slave mistress. At this time, the slave mistress was a woman known only by the name of Madam Dupre. She was about thirty five years of age and a strikingly handsome woman. She was tall and slim and carried herself with an elegant air. But her heart was made of stone and she ruled her roost with the harshness of a concentration camp capo. No slave dared challenge the word of Madam Dupre, whose talent at torture was unsurpassed.

The girls were led into the anteroom of Madam Dupre's quarters. Their coffle was unleashed and their hands unbound. After their gags had been removed, they were ordered to stand silently, their legs apart, their hands behind their heads, elbows up. The large, black guard who had led them there left without further ado.

The room was finely decorated with broad red and gold striped wallpaper, plush cushioned chairs with polished teak armrests and legs. The rug was a deep golden yellow, soft and comfortable on the girls' naked feet. There were no windows, since they were underground, but the walls contained exquisite prints of languid, sultry females, draped immodestly with only the most minimal of attire, if at all. A slave girl sat at a desk behind which stood a large oaken door. She had a telephone on the desk and was busy typing something into a computer. She paid the waiting slave girls no mind. She, like all of the females in the slave area, was naked.

After about three quarters of an hour, the telephone on the secretary's desk buzzed. She picked up the phone and answered, "Yes, mistress?" It was apparently an intercom. "Yes, mistress," she said. And again, "Yes, mistress, they're here….Yes, mistress, right away."

The secretary rose from her perch and signaled the awaiting slave girls to follow her. They were all tired and thirsty, their arms ached from their enforced position, but none dared say a word. The magnitude of the operation, its apparent machine like organization, made deviance from orders unthinkable.

Kit led the way past the oaken door that had been opened by the secretary. The girls entered a large office. A large couch and several easy chairs sat along the walls, and several ottomans were strewn around the room. The room was decorated all in blue, with a deep blue rug and light, pastel blue wallpaper. On the right side of the room was a small area where the rug had been cut back to reveal the hardwood floor beneath. A thick wooden beam stuck out from the wall about seven feet from the floor. A chain dangled from the beam with clips on its end. A small umbrella stand nearby contained an assortment of whips.

On the far end of the large room was a heavy, oaken desk. It was covered with neatly stacked papers, a telephone and some paperweights. Behind the desk sat the dark skinned, foreboding, but beautiful, Madam Dupre. She was dressed in a loosely fitting, black silk blouse, with a deep 'v' neck. The sides of her braless breasts peaked out, and her nipples pressed prominently against the soft, thin material. She wore a heavy golden chain around her neck that reached to the beginning of the swelling of her breasts. On its end dangled a pendant, a cursive, red '*k*' on a black background, surrounded by a circle of gold. The girls all noticed it and recognized its significance right away.

Dupre finished reading a memo and then placed the white paper aside. The girls were all lined up, right to left in front of the desk, several feet away. The secretary had pointed out a line taped on top of the rug and instructed the girls to place their toes on it.

The girls were seized with apprehension. It was clear that this woman was in supervisory authority of all of the many women who they had seen and many more whom they had not. They had noticed the whipping station on the side of the room and knew that it was not for show. The six naked and fearful girls stood as still as possible, each not wanting to attract the special attention of this severe looking woman.

The woman rose from her chair and circled round the desk. On her way, she picked up a thick, heavy riding crop that had been lying on her desk. The girls could she that she was wearing long, black, pleated pants and jet black high heels. She wore a large signet ring on the index finger of her left hand, containing a monogram identical to the one on her necklace. Her face was somewhat long and aquiline, in the classic Roman style. She turned her clear, steely grey eyes on her new charges. She took her time examining the six naked young women minutely. She pressed on breasts, explored the slits between their thighs, opened their mouths, pinched their bellies. When she stepped behind them, she required each one to lean over. She tested the firmness of their thighs and buttocks. When she was satisfied, she had the girls resume their standing positions and came back in front of the trembling young women, sitting on her desk, patting the palm of her hand absent mindedly with the riding crop.

"My name is Madam Dupre," she said, in a deep sensuous voice. "You are female slaves belonging to the '*k*' organization. You are all wearing the mark of your slavery and ownership on your buttocks. As slaves, you may expect that your lives will be harsh and brutal." Mary suppressed a whine at the woman's description of her future life. It confirmed her worse fears.

"You have experienced already a sampling of the pain and suffering that can be visited upon you should you fail in your duties," the woman continued. She measured each word carefully, speaking slowly and deliberately so that each word would be comprehended. It was a deliberate speech, one that she had delivered many times to new slave girls.

"Starting today, you will begin your final training to qualify as serving slaves in the large resort that you saw upstairs as you were led to this facility. You will perfect your sexual techniques, acquire luxurious deportment and be taught other skills necessary for your new roles."

Dupre paused to allow the news she had provided to sink in. It was having its intended effect. Several of the girls were crying, tears rolling down their faces. The rest projected looks of utter despair. Lana, the Hispanic beauty, was especially crushed. She had promised herself to a boy who had immigrated to the US from Mexico. They had spent the last few weeks before her departure in making hot, intensive love with each other. He had begged her not to go. She argued with him, told him that they needed the money if they were going to be together. She had promised that they would be married when she returned, practically guaranteeing him American citizenship and a future.

"You'll be able to go to school, Manuelo, get a trade," she had told him. "We can buy a house, be somebody."

Lana had grown up on the edges of Spanish Harlem in New York. Her parents barely spoke English, preferring to remain within the confines of their Hispanic neigh-borhood, watching the Spanish language shows on T.V., reading Hispanic papers. Her father was a janitor in one of the Upper East Side apartment towers, where he saw the "Americanos" living like kings. He could barely provide for his family and spent most nights sitting in front of the television drinking cheap beer. Her mother worked at a laundry a few blocks away from their tenement apartment. She seemed always tired and worn down by the world. This modeling assignment was to be Lana's big chance to earn some prestige, to take first herself, and then her family, out of the clutches of near poverty that they lived in. And to marry Manuelo, whose tender hands and soft lips drove her to heaven when they fucked.

But now, here she was, condemned to a harsher life than either of her parents had ever experienced; a lifetime away, it seemed, from her lover. Now, she felt that she had been soiled, sucking and fucking the pricks of the fierce black giants, begging and screaming for surcease when whipped, promising tearfully to give herself to them and perform any scurrilous service they demanded.

Karen still had not given up hope of freedom, although her presence in this subterranean hive made that prospect all the slimmer. No one could escape from within this huge underground bunker, that she knew. But maybe outside. "There must be boats," she thought. It was an island, after all. And there had to be some legitimate authority somewhere, some agency or government that would abhor this island of depravity enough to extinguish it. There had to be!

But right now, Karen and Lana, and all the rest were concentrating on the instructions of their new mistress, their supervisor, the agent of the mysterious organization that owned them. One missed rule, one unheard instruction could mean a world of pain.

Dupre continued. "You have learned your slave mantras. You would do well to keep them ever present in your mind. No act demanded of you will be too outrageous to perform; no trial meted out to you will be too painful to endure. You will be whipped, and worse, that goes without saying. But let me tell you this, a woman's wrath is ten times that of a man's. Woe betide you if you should ever incur mine."

The buzzer rang on her telephone. She reached back to answer it. "Yes," she said after listening to her secretary's message. "Show her in."

The door opened behind the six forlorn women. They heard the soft footsteps of high heels on the rug behind them. A naked woman approached Dupre. She was about 26 or 27 years old. She had long, braided blond hair. She wore no collar and no leather bracelets. She wore only a thick, black, leather belt around her midriff. Attached to it were a small, black baton and a many tassled whip. At its center, over the buckle, was the feared and hated crest of the '*k*' organization.

"Reporting as you desired, madam," the woman said. Her voice was clipped and hard. She ignored the six naked young women standing on her left.

"These are the new slaves for you to train. I want you to whip them all severely tonight to mark their arrival. You make take one for your use, if you like. Tomorrow I want them on a tight regimen of training and exercise. Let's get those last ounces of baby fat from them and tone up those limbs. "

"Yes, madam," the well muscled woman replied.

"All except that one," Dupre said pointing with the riding crop towards Rene. "I'll deal with her."

"Yes, madam," the blonde woman answered. And to the nervous young slave girls she said, "Turn to the right and then follow me."

Karen, Mary, Lana, Kit and Sheila passed from the room in a column, their stomachs churning with fear. They were to be beaten "severely". They all rued their upcoming ordeal.

While the five anxious, dispirited and frightened young women were marching out, Dupre was watching Rene intently. She had read the training materials on her, the background. She was a muff diver, a rug muncher. She liked it on top. She was hot headed and strong of will. "Well," Dupre thought to herself, "we'll see."

But Rene had already been truly broken. Day after day of almost incessant punishment and abuse had taken their toll. She craved obedience and desired only someone to obey. But she sensed a cruel taskmaster in the woman who was eying her exposed flesh with so much lust. Dupre let her stand there in silence for a few minutes.

"Kneel," Dupre suddenly commanded the frightened and miserable young girl. Rene knew that she had been singled out for a reason. Was she still paying for her stupid attempt at escape?

Dupre was still leaning against the desk. Rene saw her hand go to her waist and then draw down the front zipper of the pants. The pants were designed so that the zipper ran farther than just necessary for removal. The zipper descended deep within the mistress's thighs. When the buttons holding the waist together were loosened, she was able to reveal her black, bushy sex in all its glory.

"Come here and lick my cunt, slave," Dupre ordered.

Rene unhesitatingly walked between Dupre's out-stretched legs on her knees. Her hands were still behind her head. She leaned her head forward and ran her tongue along the length of Madam Dupre's hairy slit. Dupre's thighs were firm and strong and she closed them around Rene's head, locking her face into her pussy.

"Suck on my cunt, angel," she teased the girl. "Make it nice and wet."

Rene was having trouble breathing with her face and nose mashed into Dupre's pussy. It was wet and pungent and, in spite of herself, Rene began to become excited as she breathed the musky aroma. She pressed her tongue inside the older woman as far as it would go, and lapped up and down inside, scraping the roof with her tongue, looking to excite that special spot.

"Mmmmmm," Dupre said, her breath becoming heavy with lust. "You are a good cuntlicking bitch, slave girl. Keep it up."

Dupre leaned further back on her desk, supported by her hands behind her and spread her legs widely again. "Tickle my clit with your tongue, slut," she told her.

The slave girl obeyed, taking the stiff point of her tongue and flicking it against the little nub at the apex of the slave mistress's sex.

"Ohhhhhhhhhhh!" Dupre exclaimed. "Very good! Keep going, don't stop!" Dupre wriggled her hips on the desk and thrust them forwards to meet Rene's active tongue. "Ohhhhhhhhh!" she moaned again. "Take it in your mouth," she commanded, her voice rising to a crescendo. "Suck on it! Suck on it!" she yelled.

Rene obeyed her mistress's command. She sucked in the small soldier and tugged on it gently, sucking it while tantalizing its tip with her tongue. Madam Dupre leaned forward and grabbed Rene's head with her hands, jamming it into her flowing pouch. "Oh! Oh! Oh!" she cried out as her orgasm tore through her like lightening. At each convulsive spasm, she pushed hard on the head between her thighs, mashing it against her sex. She kept Rene's head imprisoned between her thighs until her orgasm had run its course. She released Rene's head then and ordered her to, "lick up all my juices. I don't want to soil my slacks."

Rene lapped up all of the mistress's discharge that she could. She felt her head pushed away once more. Her hands were still interlocked behind her head. She had not been ordered to release them.

"Oh, Rene," the sated slave mistress sighed. "You are a capable cunt licker. I think I'll keep you around for a little while."

Rene's eyes lit up. She would be spared the rapes and abuse of the upper world, the world of men. She smiled at her mistress to express her joy and her thanks.

"Get up, Rene," Dupre said, zipping up and fastening her slacks. "I want to express my thanks for your good service. Come with me." She waived Rene towards her. Near the back of the room was a heavy steel door. Dupre unlocked it with a key that dangled on a chain from her waist. She opened the door and beckoned Rene to walk through.

Rene did not know what to expect. Certainly the kind and grateful sounding tones of the mistress' voice was encouraging. But when she crossed the threshold, her heart sank. The room was lined with small cages, various well used whipping posts, a strange contraption that looked as if it were from the Middle Ages, and a four by eight steel table with rings mounted strategically around its sides. Two of the cages held women, their heads hooded. The cages were so small that Rene could see their skin poking out between the bars. In the corner of the room, a petit, blond headed girl was suspended from the ceiling. Her ankles and wrists were joined together and she had been hoisted into the air so that her body hung like a stilled pendulum. The front ring on her collar was connected by a chain to her wrists and ankles, keeping her head elevated. Every few seconds, she gave out a moan and a jump. As her body swung round, Rene could see that her ass and cunt had been stuffed with thick metal prongs and that the prongs were connected by wire to an electrical box. The shocks to her nether parts must have varied in intensity, because the next time the girl's body jolted, she gave out a long, loud scream.

Dupre closed the door behind her. "Do you like my little play room, Rene? I think that we can find something appropriate to help you relax and enjoy your new surroundings."

Rene's stomach went into a deep dive. Her hands still behind her head, she backed away from the approaching slave mistress.

"Don't be coy, Rene," she said to the distraught girl. "It'll only get you into trouble."

Reluctantly, Rene stopped retreating away from the cruel woman. Dupre grabbed her by the elbow and led her to the steel table.

"I know what we'll do, Rene," she said, taunting the girl. "I think that I'll whip your cunt. How about that?"

Rene was close to emotional breakdown. She knew it was verboten, but she could not withhold her speech. "Oh, please, madam, please don't whip me, please," she managed to whimper. Her body was shaking at the prospect of the resumption of her physical abuse.

Rene felt the hand on her arm grip her more tightly. "You know there's no talking, Rene. I'll have to give you extra lashes for that. Come on now," she said to the cringing young woman. "Hop on the table like a good little girl."

Her eyes issuing a torrent of tears, Rene managed to sit up on the table. Its surface was cool. She could see her reflection in its gleaming surface. As soon as she was perched on the table, Madam Dupre pulled her down onto her back. She guided the docilely accepting girl's arms to the top of the table where she affixed both bracelets to a ring in the middle. The black clothed mistress leaned over and stroked Rene's face. "Oh, don't cry, little one. We haven't even started yet." The older woman ran her long, boney fingers across Rene's plump breasts. "And you do have such a pretty body, my dear. Such nice breasts!" She pinched Rene's nipples harshly, drawing a moan of pain from the girl. "I can't wait to whip your tits, Rene. But maybe later. I have something else in mind for now."

Dupre went down to the foot of the table. She produced two long straps from a shelf underneath and tied one to each of Rene's ankles. She then returned to the head of the table, holding the free end of the straps in her hands. She began to pull at the straps until Rene's ankles started to rise into the air. When the girl was practically bent in two, her ankles up past her ears, Dupre tied the straps off on rings at the corners of the table. The girl's legs were spread wide and her double clefts were clearly visible. Dupre returned to the foot of the table and producing another strap, tied it around Rene's waist, pulled it tight, and then tied it off on the ring in the middle of the table's end.

"There," Dupre said almost merrily. "This way you won't fall off of the table, Rene. We want you good and still for your whipping. In fact, I think we can draw the ankles down a little more now." The tall, slender woman adjusted the ankle straps so that Rene's knees almost touched the table top. Dupre ran her cool hands down the inner portions of Rene's thighs and over her buttocks. "Oooh!" she said. "So smooth!" She placed her hand on Rene's sex.

"Should we get you a little warmed up?" she asked. Rene, miserable and afraid, remained silent. Dupre looked down at her face.

"Didn't they teach you politeness, Rene? You have to say 'If it pleases you, madam.' Come on now, say it."

Rene's mind was far away from the niceties of civil discourse. She knew that very soon she would be howling and screeching with pain. But she also knew that this cruel woman would seize on any pretext to extend her suffering. Her throat and mouth were dry with fear. Her whole body was shaking in apprehension of the blows to come. Rene managed to squeak out some words. "If it p,p,pleases you, madam," she said, her voice little above a whisper.

"Oh, it does please me, Rene. It does very much," the slave mistress replied. The sadistic woman leaned over and took Rene's clit into her mouth. She sucked on it gently while she rubbed her hands up and down Rene's pale thighs. She licked the length of Rene's moistening gash, tickling the little bud with her rigid tongue. As she moved her head back, she replaced her mouth with her hand, seizing the whole of the pudenda, rubbing and massaging the engorging lips. Dupre leaned her mouth down to near Rene's. She circled Rene's head with her free hand and placed her lips on Rene's. Rene thought briefly about refusing the tongue that was insistently pushing its way past her lips. But she knew that she was powerless to oppose the desires of this seemingly mad woman. She opened her mouth and let the woman's tongue mingle with her own. In spite of her fear, her revulsion at the touch of this cruel woman, Rene's breath began to become labored. She could feel her labia softening and distending. Her breasts were becoming tight and warm. The hand of her mistress continued its expert manipulation of her exposed sex. When she moaned, a wave of growing pleasure washing over her, she knew that she was lost. It was what Dupre had been waiting for.

"Oh, Rene," she said as she pulled her mouth from the supine girl's. "You're a hot slut. That's good. We're going to have such fun together." She released her grasp of Rene's soaking pussy and walked over to a cabinet where she removed a long birch rod, its tip tapered to a tiny point.

"I was thinking of using the tasseled whip, Rene, but your current position really calls for pinpoint accuracy," she told the trembling girl. "I wouldn't want to miss your little love canal, or the little brown rosette between your cheeks. I think that this'll do much better. Don't you Rene?" she asked, whooshing the whip through the air.

Rene, hearing the tell tale sound of the whip being prepared for use, could hold back her piteous entreaties no longer. "Oh, please, mistress!" she cried in an anguished voice. "I'll do anything you say! Anything! Please don't whip me, please!"

"That's it Rene," Dupre answered. "You'll be screaming like mad in a second anyway. Cry out all you want."

Rene began to blubber and wail as she anticipated the cruel blows that she was about to suffer. Madam Dupre moved to the girl's side.

"I think I'll get a better shot at your cunt from the side, Rene. Let's see if I can land the tip of the whip right on your clit." The tall, well toned woman drew the whip back and lashed out with all of her strength. She swung the whip with a backhand stroke and its tip landed just below Rene's love bud. "Crack!'

"Ahhhhhhhhhhhhhhhh!" the poor girl cried. She jerked and strained at her bonds as the pain wrenched her body. The kiss of the whip felt like a knife had been plunged into her loins.

"Ah, Rene," Dupre shouted with glee. "Right on the money. Let's see if I can do it again."

While Rene moaned and cried, begging for mercy, Dupre brought the whip back again and once more swung it backhand towards the girl's burning loins." 'Crack!'

She struck Rene's clit dead center. "Aiyeeeeee!" the girl screeched. "Oh, god! Oh god!" she yelled. Her little bud emitted a whole world of pain through her body. She desperately tried to bring her legs together, to protect her loins from the cruel abuse.

"Let's try your little brown star nest, Rene. I bet that'll hurt like the blazes."

The supple and lithe woman returned to the head of the table. "Oh this is an easy shot, Rene," she said. "Just up and down. But let's see how hard I can hit it."

Rene tried to steel herself for the next blow. She gathered up all of her courage as she saw the whip rise. She closed her eyes tightly to block out the sight of its descent. Dupre brought it down swiftly, putting her weight into it. 'Crack!'

Rene's voice had grown hoarse with screaming. Her wail was almost guttural. The impact of the whip's tip on her pursed rear lips was electrifying. Her body convulsed in pain. Her anguished voice echoed through the small torture chamber. Ten more blows the slave mistress inflicted on Rene's body. Her wailing and moaning was almost deafening. The woman struck her dainty rear ring again and then marched the whip up and down the inside of her thighs.

When she was finished, Madam Dupre had worked up quite a sweat. Rene was in a whirlwind of pain. She moaned and groaned, muttering futile pleas. Dupre took stock of herself. "Ah, Rene, that was wonderful. I think I'll go take a shower and get one of your friends to lick my pussy. I've worked up quite a lust. You've been very cooperative. I'm going to let you hang out here a while. I'll be back a little later and then we can start on your luscious tits." Before leaving, Dupre shoved a leather gag into Rene's moaning mouth. There was no talking between slaves permitted in Madam Dupre's dungeon. The slave mistress patted Rene on her backside. "See you soon, slave," she said. And then she left.

CHAPTER EIGHT
THE WAGES OF SIN

Nicholai Kodar sat drinking his tonic with lime. It was a sunny afternoon. The daily afternoon showers had fled and the sun had burst out again, causing steam to rise from the roofs of the neighboring cottages. He was on the shade porch that sat on a small hill that overlooked Klitzman's resort and he could note the hustle and bustle of the place as blue, black and brown robed creatures darted back and forth. It was like watching ants.

He had in his hand his bank's confirmation of receipt of a draft for 1.25 million dollars; his share of the 3.75 mil Klitzman had recovered on the plane. There was another $270,000 bonus for bringing in the girls. $30,000 each. Not bad.

He was leaving in a little while and had just one more piece of business to take care of. He rose from his chair, downed the tonic. Nicholai never drank alcohol. It dulled the senses and clouded the mind. He wanted to be in control and at his peak all the time.

The facilities on the island that were made available to supervisors depended a lot upon status. The rough and tumble street guys usually had their stay confined to the supervisors' dormitory. High achievers, like Nicholai, were allotted cottages, five room units with a full bath and a fully stocked 'playroom' where slaves could be maltreated. The cottages, built on a rise that ascended from the main plateau, were ranked by view. Nicholai's cottage had an ocean view and a view of the resort. Others overlooked the golf course. Some had no view to speak of at all. All in all there were twenty cottages, some reserved permanently for use by specific individuals who might spend significant time at the resort and temporary ones, like the one Nicholai occupied. He had made a big score and had risen in the Klitzman firmament.

Above the cottages, were the mansions. There were four of them. One were occupied by Cholo and Thorndike. Anthony occupied another and two were reserved for the use of royalty, presidents and other heads of state and their guests.

Although smaller than the many roomed mansions, the cottages were not to be sneezed at. The living room was sunken with a large flat panel T.V., a wet bar. There, too, were the necessities of slave abuse, a whipping post, an ottoman surrounded by iron rings. The kitchen was fully stocked and a servant usually assigned to do the cooking. There was a well appointed dining room and a spacious bedroom. Cottage residents were privileged to have slaves assigned to them on long term basis. The slaves were expected to clean and straighten out the house, and wait patiently the return of their masters.

The veranda ran off of the living room and when Nicholai entered it he saw a pair of cringing, woeful eyes staring back at him. They belonged to a skinny, long haired brunette, with long, slinky legs and tea cup breasts. Her body bore long, thick red welts all across it, with deep purple bruises on her thighs, breasts and ass. She was sitting in the middle of the floor. Her arms had been fed under her legs and then her wrists were affixed to the outside of her ankles. In this posture, the slave was unable to close her legs. There were tight, sharp clamps on her tormented nipples, the lips of her vagina and over the little nubbin at its top. One final clamp gripped her tongue tightly, forcing it to be maintained outside of her mouth.

The girl's eyes were red rimmed and her face was a picture of abject fear. Nicholai stopped to regard her. He had enjoyed abusing this cunt. She had been his for the last three days. Three days was about the limit that any slave girl could ordinarily take with him. Word must have gotten around because this girl had been crying when she was delivered.

But Nicholai did not have time to linger. There were things to do before he left. He had about three hours before the seaplane he had chartered would take him to his own little island resort about four miles off of the Cuban coast. He had performed great services for the revolutionary government there and was left well enough alone. He had a staff of three servants and two slave girls waiting for him. He was sure that the slave girls were in no rush to see him again. But, hey, life was tough all over.

* * * * * * * * * * * * * * * *

Brenda was still in her cell in Rukimo's dungeon when the other girls were led away. She, of course did not know they had left because her hood prevented her from seeing or hearing what went on around her. If she was attentive, she could feel the vibration through the floor when cell doors were slammed shut. She had not sensed them being opened and shut for some time. In fact, she had gone through three feedings without being used by the trainers.

She was lying down now, chained to her cot. The hissing in her ears prevented any concentrated effort of thought, but she knew enough to realize that the routine had changed.

Suddenly, she felt through the vibration of her bed frame the opening and closing of her cell door. Hands released her ankles and wrists, which had been chained to the cot. She was lifted to her feet, her wrists fastened behind her and escorted out of the cell. Her hood and gag were left in place.

Usually, the hood and gag were removed while in the cell, and Brenda wondered why it had been left on as she was frog marched through the door that led to the training area. But they did not stop at the training area door. They were heading further down the hall. She felt herself brought to a halt, paused, and then through a doorway. She was led along the hallway to another door. She felt the unmistakable sensation of an elevator rising.

The blind and deaf girl was led along one of the winding brick pathways of the resort. She had no idea what was around her, but she did sense, from time to time along her walk, the heat of other bodies passing her, a slight wind as they went by.

Finally, they came to a stop, a door was opened, and she was led into some kind of structure. The tall African handed her leash to a white coated medical technician. "Two hours," was all he said to the black robed man. He nodded back and left.

Brenda was led down a short hallway and into a little room. The lab tech, after releasing her wrists, settled her into the chair in the center of the room. It was constructed like a dentist's or barber's chair. It had clamps on the arms, to which Brenda's wrists were quickly affixed, and for the legs. Brenda had never felt so vulnerable. Something was happening or going to happen to her and she didn't think that she was going to like it.

When the tech removed Brenda's hood, she blinked her eyes rapidly to get the adjusted to the lights. The room was stark white, much like an operating theater. There were various instruments lying about the room and a glass doored closet containing medications and medical books. Brenda was still gagged, and she shifted her weight nervously in the chair as she looked around. The techie was examining her body clinically, using his hand to examine her breasts and nipples, taking hold of her nose and looking on either side of her face. He pushed a button and the legs of the chair began to spread open. When it was wide enough, he insinuated himself between them and, kneeling down, made a visual and physical inspection of her sex.

The tech man was young, no more than twenty four or twenty five. He had a boyish face and dirty blond hair cut short, but long on top so that he had to keep tossing his head to keep it from his eyes. He stood just about Brenda's height, 5'6". In the midst of all of her trepidation, Brenda found herself thinking that he was kind of cute. The she realized that this stripling was a part of the gang of men who had kidnapped her and her friends, and who had subjected her to what seemed like weeks and weeks of abuse. Her nervousness and sense of dread returned quickly.

Brenda's collar was affixed to the back of the chair, so she couldn't turn around, but she heard a familiar sound behind her. It was the high pitched whine of an electric razor. "What would they be doing with that?" she thought. And then it hit her. "Not my hair! Oh, no, please, not my hair!"

She tried to pull her wrists from their confines, but to no avail. As the buzzing got closer, she began to waive her head back and forth, groaning through her gag to frustrate the young man's intent. But she felt a firm hand grasp the ring on the outside of her gag and hold her head steady, pulling it back until she was looking at the ceiling. She felt the razor placed against her scalp and gave one last, agonized "Noooooooooo!" through her gag. When she felt the razor run down the middle of her head, sweeping all of the hair in its path away, she surrendered to her fate.

It took the technician less than two minutes to razor off all of Brenda's beautiful auburn locks. When the last clump hit the floor, he turned off the razor and went to the sink and prepared a small bowl of steaming hot water. Brenda's head was covered with a rough stubble. She was too despondent to protest the removal of her hair's remnants. Using a straight edged razor, the man skillfully scraped away every last vestige of hair on Brenda's head.

Brenda was crying. She loved her thick reddish brown hair. Once, she had let it grow down to her waist when she was younger. But she liked to keep it the way it had been when she had gotten selected for the modeling job, slightly longer than shoulder length. She had a habit of twirling a lock of it when she was deep in thought and she liked to brush it a hundred times before going to bed each night, a kind of mind clearing, mesmerizing ritual. She liked the way that she could make herself look little girlish by putting it in pigtails. She liked it when her boyfriends ran their hands through it or when girlfriends complimented her on it. But now it was gone. Why? She didn't know. Had the other girls had their heads shaved? Was it some kind of ritual that she had to go through? She could see her reflection in a mirror that hung on the wall opposite her chair. Was it strategically placed there so that newly shaved girls could appreciate their new bald look? Brenda didn't know the answers to these questions. She just stared at her naked, boney head and cried.

She felt the man rubbing some kind of cream onto her head. It stung a little, but left her scalp feeling cool. Brenda didn't know that the cream was a depilatory agent. Applied regularly, it slowed the growth of hair. Applied three times a day for several weeks, it killed the hair roots completely.

The tech guy paused in his work. The next phases of the job would be a little more discomforting to the naked young woman sitting before him. He did his job well, and he enjoyed fucking the girls, but he was not really one of those guys who liked hurting them. But it was a job and the side benefits were outrageous.

He stepped up to the chair and cranked it down. Brenda felt her torso being lowered. Once lowered, the man pulled straps from the side of the chair and bound her torso in tightly. Brenda looked up at him with wide, supplicating eyes. "What are you going to do to me?" they seemed to ask, reflecting what Brenda had in her panicked mind.

The man went back to the counter and retrieved a small tray. The tray attached to the arm of the chair. Brenda couldn't see what was on it, because her head was too low. There was a small bowl of alcohol, a long steel rod with a sharpened tip and two large gleeming steel rings. The tech man snapped on two surgical gloves.

Brenda screamed when the tech man pierced her left nipple. She screamed again when he pierced the right. She almost didn't notice the thick rings pushed through the holes at the base of her teats. They both had a spring mechanism and when threaded through the bloody gaps that the man had made in Brenda's body, they clicked shut.

When the man did her labia, threading six thin stainless steel rings on each side, Brenda bucked and writhed in her chair. But the man had done this before and she was adequately secured before he started. He had shaved off all of her pubic hair, what little there was after her bikini trim, and applied some of the salve.

The man spent some time cleaning up the blood that had spilled from Brenda's wounds. She sat moaning into her gag, squirming her hips at the continuing pain. The holes would heal soon enough, but for at least the next eighteen hours or so, they would burn and sting every time the rings were touched.

Next to come was the mouth. For this part, for very practical reasons, the policy was to administer a soporific. He would give her something that would make her woozy and unable to do more than mumble and murmur, but she would still be aware of what was being done to her. It was best that a slave personally experience every stage of her debasement.

The tech man rubbed a small circle of alcohol in the nape of Brenda's arm and injected the solution. It would take about fifteen minutes to really slow her down and so he went outside for a smoke.

As her mind began to fog, Brenda was wallowing in self pity. She couldn't understand why this was happening to her. She had always been good. She hadn't been mean to anyone. She had been home promptly at twelve when she was younger. She had joined the public service organization at her suburban Jersey high school. She didn't drink or smoke or do drugs. Then why was she being punished? Why were these things happening to her? As her mind floated, visions of her recent torments ran through her mind. She had screamed with pain when whipped, and cowered at the mere thought of it. She had hated the cruel penetration of her body by the harsh black men. She had hated herself when they had forced her to pleasure. She would never get used to it. Never!

When the techie returned, Brenda's eyes were rolled back, her face, slack. He removed her gag. She noticed when he pulled it out, attempting speech. She emitted only a slight mumble. A leather band was wrapped around the top of her head to hold it in place against the headrest. Clamps were pushed up against the sides of her head to keep it still. The man looked at Brenda's pretty mouth. She had plump, almost bee stung lips. He leaned over and kissed them, running his tongue along the underside, taking in her hot breath. "She's a sweet one," he thought to himself. He took a moment to contemplate what he was about to do. "Well, fuck it," he said aloud, finally.

He stood up and retrieved another tray from the counter. After donning another pair of surgical gloves, he unwrapped a strange, round device from its cellophane packaging. The device had two circles of plastic, one hard and one soft. There was a little ridge between them. The techie took up the device and brought it to Brenda's mouth. Against her mumbled protest, he pushed it inside. Brenda's teeth fell squarely inside the gap between the circles. The soft side of the device, a little thicker than the other, lay against the back of Brenda's teeth. The front was set between her teeth and her gums. There were small holes all around the hard plastic circle. The tech man examined the fit of the device closely. It was perfect.

Brenda didn't know it, but she was fitted for the device a week before. She had assumed that the thick, round plug of clay that had been forced between her lips had been yet one more dehumanizing torture. She had been blinded by her hood, and could not see what was happening when they pressed her jaw up against the clay and pressed her lips against it. After it was carefully removed, her gag was replaced. The tart taste of the clay remained in her mouth for hours.

There was no sense removing the device once it was in. The techie picked up a specially designed tool and brought it to Brenda's mouth. It was somewhat like a leather puncher The man placed part of it behind Brenda's gums, behind the circle of plastic and, finding a hole, closed the handles, punching a hole the width of a ten penny nail in her gum. The tool had also inserted a steel plug through the hole. Brenda gurgled in pain. The techie, while holding the tool in place, picked up a small, round ball from a dish on the tray. The ball had a small opening and he placed it on the portion of the tool head that was outside Brenda's mouth and then clamped the tool shut once again. There was a click as the rod married itself to the ball. The two pieces were lodged together almost inseparably. They met just on the upper portion of Brenda's lip, directly under her nose.

Brenda moaned and whined as the man fiddled with her mouth. She protested distractedly as she felt the sting of another hole being punched through her skin above her lip. Her clouded mind could not fathom what was being done. She tried to shake her head, but it was too tightly confined and she was too weak from the drug.

The rest of the holes went just as easy. The only difficulty was to get the lips pursed just right as the circle around them was completed. He had installed a vacuum tube in the girl's mouth to carry away the saliva and blood. When he was finished, Brenda's lips were surrounded by a circle of small, shiny, steel balls. Her mouth was fixed open in a small circle, just the size of a man's cock. The lips themselves were left loose so that they could drag against the shaft as the cock rode back and forth. But since the lips would no longer be able to grasp the cock tightly, the device was really designed for throat fucking. There was no need to order the girl to "open up". There was no danger of her clasping her jaws shut in panic as she fought for air. And when the mouth was not in use, there was a specially designed gag that fit nicely over the little balls to seal it tightly in.

Of course her meals would all, from now on, be pureed. There was no chance that she would be able to chew anything. And, sadly, as least in the techie's opinion, she had been given her last kiss. He looked at the girl, her jaw slack, her mouth rounded as if a cock were already present as he considered the next step. It would be fairly easy as it was pretty much straight forward.

He reached into Brenda's gaping mouth with a small pincer. He trapped her tongue and dragged it out of her mouth, extending it to its full length. A clamp was pressed together, running across the base of the tongue, wider than her mouth, keeping the tongue trapped outside.

He quickly installed four little round balls on either side of her tongue. Brenda jumped slightly as each hole was made. When done, there were four little round steel balls on her tongue, which she would find useful when caressing the shaft of her master as he raped her mouth. The tongue was released and returned to Brenda's mouth. Adding a nose ring was simple and he soon had the thick, gleaming steel ring inserted. It clicked against the balls on the top of Brenda's upper lip when he released it.

The poor girl was just starting to come out of her stupor. She would soon be in excruciating pain. She would struggle and sob about the violence done to her mouth. But she would not be able to speak a single word of protest although her mouth was wide open.

The techie now worked quickly. He unlocked her wrists from the arms of the chair and pulled her out of it. Brenda was unsteady on her feet as he led her across the room. There was a low, padded table there and the techie laid her across it, face down. He quickly unlocked and removed her leather bracelets. He taped her wrists together, palms facing each other, and began to install a heavy, leather sleeve over her arms. He pulled it down to the base of the arms and expertly began to lace it up. Brenda's arms were brought tightly together. She moaned and began to squirm slightly. She moaned harder when he folded her arms backwards, and pressed her wrists firmly against her back. Laces at the very tip of the sleeve ran through a ring at the edge of the lower portion, which was now up around Brenda's shoulder blades. He pulled it tight through that ring and tied it off.

As Brenda was beginning to moan and cry with the pain to her mouth and arms, the man removed her thick, leather collar and replaced it with a heavy, black, steel one. It closed up against her neck tightly, its inside coated with a soft foam. But it was wider than the leather collar and there was a little wedge in the front that forced the head up. It too had spring locks and when the heavy collar was clamped closed, it was removable only with the use of an acetylene torch. Two straps from the leather sleeve were tied off on the ring at the back of the collar.

Two heavy circlets of blackened steel were affixed to Brenda's ankles and her new uniform was complete. She was beginning to regain her senses and the techie figured that it was time for her to admire his handiwork. He pulled her up to a standing position and led her to the full length mirror. Brenda looked up and began to wail. She saw her deformed body before her, her grotesque mouth, the rings through her nipples and nose. She felt the intense pain on her tongue and stuck it out only to see the tiny, little shiny balls inserted there. Her hairless head made her seem subhuman.

Tears poured from the young girl's eyes. She tried to protest the maiming of her body, but all that emerged from her mouth were gurgling sounds. The young man leaned over and put his fingers through the rings along her labial lips, pulling on them slightly. The pain drew Brenda's attention there and her wailing began anew.

"What cruel, depraved person would do this to me?" she thought piteously. Her knees weakened as the enormity of what had been done to her sank in. She was to be somebody's toy, not a person at all. All of her personality had been removed. The techie clipped a chain to the ring in the front of her collar and led her from the room.

He sat her down on a chair in the anteroom, strapping her in place. She was still moaning in pain and profound despair. The techie picked up the telephone and dialed a number. "Hello," he said. He waited. "Yeah, this is Custom Detailing. She's ready."

Brenda wondered fearfully who she could be ready for. She could not imagine the cruelty of a man who would have this done to her. What would he do to her once he took possession of her? How much would she suffer? Would she ever be free and whole again?

The techie had draped a black bag loosely over Brenda's head while she awaited her new, cruel master. After an agonizing, interminable wait, she heard the door open and then heard a familiar voice say, "Let me see her."

She was brought to her feet and the bag lifted. She could not believe her eyes. It was Paderovski! The man who had betrayed them! The man who she had thought about in bed at night, dreaming of his falling in love with her, making love to her! And now he was right there in front of her. She tried to back away from him, crying out, "No! No!" It sounded more like "Oh! Oh!"

Nicholai, aka Paderovski, grabbed the girl by the ring on the front of her collar. He pulled her to himself. He smiled at her, a cold, deadly smile. His eyes, which had always seemed to Brenda to be full of life, had turned black as a shark's.

"Come here, Brenda," he said in a sing song voice. "Let me take a look at you. You sure look different than when the last time I saw you. I think you're more to my taste now."

He shifted his grip to the steel rings that pierced Brenda's ample breasts. "Ooooghf!" she cried as she tried to protest the pain. He lifted her up on to her toes. Brenda screeched in pain.

"Now, now, my little slut, you'll soon experience pain a lot worse than this. What will you do then, huh?"

Brenda's stomach sank; it was as if a heavy load had just landed on her body. "Oh, God," she pleaded in her mind. "How will I ever survive it? Why did he pick me? Why? Why? Why?"

It was as if he was reading her mind, a thought that increased Brenda's dread. "You know, Brenda, I could have had any one of you girls. Kit and Sheila were prettier. And Karen had bigger tits, and whiter skin. No, although you were beautiful too, Brenda, I picked you because you seemed the one best suited to suffering. I saw that right away. I dreamed of laying a lash on your body. And soon, I will. But right now, I want to give my new slave girl a fuck."

Nicholai looked up at the tech man who shrugged. "Be my guest," he said.

The cruel, heartless man dragged Brenda over to a table at the side of the room. He threw her back against it and, lifting her legs, forced her down on it. Brenda was shrieking and protesting. "This can't be real!" she thought as he spread her legs apart. "This can't be happening!"

Nickolai was wearing his street clothes and took the time to release his steel hard cock from his pants. When it was freed, he pushed his body between Brenda's legs. He circled his arms under her thighs and lifted them up until the crux of her knees were resting on his forearms. He reached in to Brenda's cunt and grabbed the rings that pierced her labia. Brenda screamed in pain as he pulled them apart, revealing the soft pink interior of her slit. He pressed his cock against the length of the slit, teasing it, conveying his heat to it. He leaned forward and was able to insinuate the tip of his rod inside the opening of Brenda's pussy. He was determined to take his time. He had waited weeks for this. No girl left Klitzman's isle without training, and Brenda was no exception. She bore Klitzman's mark, imposing his ultimate and superior right to her.

Brenda shuddered as she felt the hard cock begin to force its way inside her. It was like a poisonous leach possessing her. She yearned to shut her nether lips tightly, to prevent his entrance. But instead, her lips were being pulled widely apart, rendering vulnerable the crevasse between them.

Slowly, but surely, Nicholai exercised his cock in Brenda's tight hole. Against her will, the friction began to draw her cunt into lubrication. It was like a geometric progression. The deeper he penetrated her sheath, the more excited it became, the more it yearned to be filled. Nicholai pressed his cock gently forwards, until suddenly all resistance faded, and it slid easily in. Brenda's body quailed as she felt the cruel man fill her. She had orgasmed for the black men, they had shown her that she was weak, that she could not resist her own urges. Even now she could feel the heat building in her loins.

Her master began pumping harder now, his own lust creeping higher and higher. He pulled on the rings, evoking a moan of pain from the girl. He thrust his hips again and again against hers, his urgency beginning to crest. But he wanted to wait, knew that he could. He wanted to see Brenda's now bizarre face cringe as her cunt's spasms flew through her. She started to push her hips against his, started a low, steady moan. Her eyes opened and she began to hoot through her grotesquely formed mouth. "Ooooooooooooo!" she called. "Ooooooooooooo!"

At the strange sounds of Brenda's orgasm, Nicholai released his torrent of spewm into her. Her cunt grabbed him tightly as it convulsed. "Ahhhhhhhh!" he yelled as he shot his load into the supine girl. "Ahhhhhhhh!"

When his balls had emptied themselves fully into the girl's womb, Nicholai withdrew his softening meat from Brenda's still shuddering cunt. He looked at her face. She was crying softly.

He left the girl lying on the table. He obtained from the techie a thick, leather cord. He quickly looped it inside the rings on Brenda's labia, criss-crossing them, and then pulling the lips tightly closed. Brenda moaned in pain at the pressure on the still sore rings. She could feel him tying off the cord. The point was obvious. Her cunt was not her own. It was his. He could have it anytime he wanted, but she wouldn't be able to even touch it.

Nicholai looked on at his new slave. He had others, but nothing compared to the feeling of acquiring a new one. It was probably time for the older one he kept at his island to go anyway. He would devise a delicious send off for her. "Maybe Klitzman is right," he thought as he watched the forlorn expression of the slave girl in front of him. "Too much is never enough."

There was that idea he had talked over with that Cuban intelligence agent last month. Many beautiful, vibrant, young girls applied for careers in the intelligence service. Some had to be sent on dangerous missions. Some would certainly perish in service to the state. Say maybe fifteen or twenty a year? More? He could trade some of them to Klitzman for some Norte Americano girls or some Swedes. Those Cuban guys liked Swedes.

Brenda felt herself pulled to her feet. She looked around for someone to save her from this monster, but the tech man was busy with some paperwork. Nicholai called over to him. "Hey, you forgot the eyebrows."

The man looked over at the girl. "So I did," he responded. "Wait a sec."

He ran into the room in which he had performed Brenda's modifications and emerged with the electric razor. He plugged it in and it came to life. Nicholai held the girl as the man zipped the tiny lines of hair from over the girl's eyes. The techie rubbed the ointment where her eyebrows had been and handed the large container to Nicholai. "Twice a day for three weeks," he said.

Nicholai took another look at his newly acquired slave girl. That was better. There was a face devoid of almost all humanity. She could evoke pity, but not sympathy. He grabbed the girl by the ring on her collar and pulled her from the room. He had a plane to catch.

CHAPTER NINE
EAST IS EAST

The five girls soon became acclimated to the routine at the slave quarters. They were used to not seeing the sun from their time in the training dungeon anyway. They were too frightened to talk to one another. They just did what they were told and absorbed what occasional suffering was meted out to them. The oddest thing was the almost virtual silence, especially in light of the fact that well over two hundred souls could be found in the slave facility at one time or another. Talking was strictly forbidden. Orders yelled out by the slave supervisors, passionate moans, and screams and cries while at the end of a whip, didn't count. Yet slaves will have their ways and, while no one was looking, the girls would often pass news or gossip quietly between them.

Mary and the others all wondered what had happened to the other girls. Carol, Danielle and Brittany had disappeared right away. Brenda had trained with them, but must have been taken somewhere else. Rene had come down the elevator with them, but hadn't been seen since.

The training was not too rigorous. They practiced fellatio on plastic models, learned to dip and bow gracefully. They were instructed in various ways to pleasure a man and taught how to render their bodies supple to offer their masters the various poses in which sexual congress can take place. There was a well equipped exercise room and they were able to work out some of their frustrations there. And they made love. Not to each other. There was little choice permitted in sexual partners. They would be assigned a lover and be required to service and be serviced by her for the edification of their sister slaves who were instructed to watch. From time to time, one of the guards from 'upstairs' came down, or one of the higher ranking supervisors, and he would choose a girl and go to the guest rooms. Red headed, milky skinned Karen had been there twice.

And there was their slave supervisor. Each of them had spent at least one or two nights with her. Her name was Giselle, and she was Austrian. She was 27 years old and had been brought to Klitzman's island when she was 19. She valued her role as a slave supervisor, and no charge of hers was ever going to give the masters reason to send her back into the slave pool. Due to her age, she knew the next stop would likely be the soldier's barracks or a bordello in some third world slum. Klitzman took few chances, and aging out slaves were never sent anywhere where they were likely to emerge to tell their tale.

Other than having a harsh taskmaster, the girls' days were kind of mild. They exercised, they trained, they fucked. And they dreaded the day when they would be sent upstairs to serve in the resort. It was not just the fact that they feared falling short of standards, although that weighed on their minds heavily. And it was not because they feared the beatings and whippings that they had heard was commonplace. It was more because that until they had been sent up to the resort and had to preen and sway their hips, appear inviting to all, pretend lust for men they would consider gross and repellant, until then they were still not whores. Until they had to pretend lust, to entice men to their use, to fawn over them and give out an aura of willing, wanton sluts, there remained part of them that was still unsullied. They did now only what they had to, what they were ordered to do. Upstairs, if men considered them unworthy of use, they would quickly be deemed unworthy of service and shipped off to more undesirable fates.

This had been explained to them many times since they had been brought to the Slave Center. It had sunk in.

Mary had gotten so used to the routine that one day she actually found herself humming as she bathed one of the other slaves. The girl, an older woman, no neophyte to slavery, smiled and turned and kissed her. It was nice. Afterwards, she felt depressed and ashamed that she could ever get used to being a naked, propertyless, rightless non-entity.

One day, Mary and four other newly enslaved girls were called to the guest rooms. Karen was one of them. Their numbers had been called over the intercom, numbers that they had been trained to learn by heart. It was the same number that was printed and coded on their collars, so that a simple swipe of an electronic wand would record their comings and goings at various places in the resort. The wand never lied and God help the girl who tarried while traveling their well timed routes.

The guest area had a large lounge, much like one of the lounges upstairs. There were two or three girls assigned to it daily and they would serve drinks and refreshments to any visitor. When Mary entered, there were already three slave girls standing in a line, their heads downcast, legs apart, their hands behind their backs. As she joined them, she saw a tall Asian man sitting in an armchair. Next to him sat the slave mistress, Madam Dupre. He was drinking a tall, cool, clear liquid. A serving slave knelt on the floor just behind him and to his right, prepared to fulfill any and all of his desires.

It was a few moments before the fifth girl entered, to the visible ire of Madam Dupre. When she was standing in the line, Mary noticed that Madam Dupre had a kind of notebook on her lap. The slave mistress stood once all the slaves had appeared and invited the oriental man to inspect them.

He was dressed in black pants, white running shoes and a knitted green sports shirt. He had a small beard on his chin. He seemed young to be a colonel, but he carried himself with the air of self assurance that command brings. He had been wearing sunglasses, but when he rose, he took them off. He was unusually tall for an Asian, and the females, all except Madam Dupre, seemed to diminish in stature before him.

"These are the slaves you selected, Colonel," Madam Dupre said as the man stepped towards them. "Let me have them step out so you can examine them. You've read their backgrounds, but if you have any questions, I have their profiles right here."

Mary felt nauseous as she realized that this man was probably going to buy one or more of them. She had heard that that was possible. Some of the girls who were taken away actually returned. After retraining, they would mix with the general population. Their stories were never pretty.

There was at least a 20% chance that she would be chosen. Her mind raced. He was a military man, a colonel. She knew that in some countries in Asia, the military was so corrupt that it was treated more like a business. Was he shopping for some fat, lecherous general? Or was he looking to fill some special order for a brothel? Was he looking for himself? He was only a colonel. But what did she know, Mary thought. He could be a multimillionaire.

Karen had made the same connection as Mary. Of all the girls kidnapped by Paderovski, she was the one with the largest breasts, the whitest skin. She had unusual red hair, naturally red, as the man could clearly see. She would be as exotic to an Asian as an Indian would be to an Eskimo. She had no desire to be shipped out to some Asian hinterland. She still harbored a fantasy about escaping the island on a boat. She knew boats. Her father had been a fisherman off the Long Island Sound. He had gone for swordfish and tuna. On occasion, she would go with him. Her mother divorced him because he was a brutal drunk. But at sea, he was her father, the master of the sea. And she knew the sea, at least well enough to get many miles away from where they were. And she knew some elementary navigation. She just needed a chance to get upstairs and slip away. She would find the boats. She would escape.

But not if this cruel looking man took her far away to some Asian jungle. And she heard that the oriental men could be especially cruel. She tried not to look at him, to become unnoticed, to disappear right in front of him.

The other three girls were nervous too. They had just come down from training the day before. They were still jumping at every noise, cringing at every command. The colonel was looking for fresh meat, girls new to their slavery. Trained, but not passed around.

One by one, Dupre called the girls forward. The first girl was a dark skinned Italian girl. She had little English, but knew enough to obey Dupre's obvious hand signals. Dupre snapped her fingers and the girl raised her arms behind her head in obedience. The colonel grabbed her cheeks with his large hand and stared into her eyes. Mary could see the girl trembling. He moved her head from side to side, looking for flaws. He stepped back and placed his hands on her breasts, measuring them, watching the girl's reactions. He pinched the nipples harshly, causing the girl to wince and emit a feint whine. He smiled.

"Lovely," he said, his voice high pitched, the vowels drawn out. "Please to turn around," he told the girl. Her name was Annette. She had made the mistake of going out for cigarettes at about 2 A.M. one night. She was at her boyfriend's who lived in a rather rough neighborhood in Naples. The all night store was only three blocks away. She got the cigarettes, but didn't make it back to her boyfriend's apartment. He was passed out from drugs and alcohol and didn't realize that she wasn't there until ten o'clock the next morning. He assumed she had gone back to her place; her roommates assumed that she was with him. By the time anyone missed her, she was lying, bound and drugged, deep in the bowels of a large freighter heading to South America. One of Klitzman's speedboats met it a couple miles off of the Canary Islands. From there she, and two other fine Italian girls, were flown to Klitzman's island.

Madam Dupre gave a little twirl of her fingers and the girl understood the command. She turned her back to the colonel presenting her smooth, well toned buttocks to his view. He ran his hands down her back and across her hips. He felt the flesh of her rear globes. He placed one hand on the girl's stomach and pressed firmly on her back. She leaned over in response. Her legs were already spread and the Asian was able to place his hand on her fleshy mound. He ran his hand along the inside of her thighs, caressing the smooth skin. His fingers found her slit, and he gently nudged the lips apart. After a few moments, his efforts were rewarded as the girl's juices began to flow. She had been taught well.

The colonel manipulated the folds of the girl's sex, the bud at the tip of the lips, the now juicy interior. He waited until her breath began to deepen and she uttered a small moan. He then reached around and took hold of her dangling, pale breasts. He felt the stiff nipples, the firmness of the twin mounds. He pulled her back up and spun her around, looking again into her face, observing the young woman in heat.

Annette was ordered back into the line and the next girl was ordered forward. One by one, he examined them all in the same way. When done, he strolled back and forth along the line of fearful women, touching a breast here, reexamining a pussy there.

Madam Dupre watched the man patiently. His name was Colonel Huong. He was Cambodian. He represented a general who controlled a heavily traveled route for the smuggling of raw opium out of Thailand. The general had begun to experiment with his own crop as well and the colonel had just delivered twenty ounces of their new product as a sample of its quality. Klitzman, in a gesture of good will, had offered the colonel to return to Cambodia with a gift for the general. The colonel risked losing much face if he made a poor choice. He had poured over thirty or forty pictures of newly enslaved girls and had reduced his choice to these five. Any one would be acceptable. But only one was the best.

"Please," he said to Madam Dupre, "may I look at these two again?"

He had pointed to Karen and a lithe, blond haired Czech girl. He had them stand side by side. Karen's breasts were ample and plump, her nipples wide and flat. Her hips were just a little wide, and her mouth, when at rest, just a tad down turned. But she had beautiful brown eyes, hazel, actually, a slender, pert nose and a feint smattering of freckles on her cheeks.

The other girl, Zelenka, was tall and thin. Her breasts were heavy for her frame, round and firm, like half melons. She had star-like blue eyes. Her hair was short and curly, almost in ringlets. He nose was long and narrow, her eyes set close together. She was maybe a little too thin, the colonel thought to himself. Her ass was a little boney. But she had dazzling eyes and her form was graceful, luxurious. He sent both girls back into the line.

"That one," he said, pointing at Mary. While Karen breathed a sigh of relief, Mary's heart skipped. "Oh, god," she thought, "he's going to pick me!"

Mary's skin was a light pastel pink. She had shoulder length black hair, deep blue eyes. Her breasts were almost as large as Karen's, but whereas Karen's were thick and heavy, hers were wide and firm. Her stiff nipples, stiff from fear, were long, but not thin. There was a small mole on her right breast just below and to the right of her nipple. Her areolas were smooth and half dollar sized. She had thin lips, a slightly broad nose. Her eyelashes were dark and thick, giving her face a brooding look. If any of the girls had a mysterious air about her it was Mary. Her mien bespoke the poetess, a seducer of men. She did not help her cause by tilting her head slightly downward, keeping her tear brimming eyes firmly focused on the floor a few feet ahead.

The colonel felt her breasts again and tugged at her narrow, trimmed black bush. It was truly a hard decision. He stood, his hand under his chin, the fingers of his other hand nervously tapping on his thigh. He turned to Madam Dupre.

"I have decided,' he said. Mary almost feinted. The colonel raised his hand and pointed. "That one," he said.

His finger was pointing directly at Karen. She had been right. Her bright orange hair and her milky white, plump breasts had won the day. The general was no poet, much to the colonel's dismay. For himself, he would have chosen Mary.

Karen's eyes widened with shock and panic at the colonel's selection. She lost control of herself. Gone was all hope of escape. Wherever this man was from, it would be far, far away. "No!" she screamed. She ran for the door, pushing the colonel out of her way. She had no place to go, she knew that. And her punishment was sure to be severe. But all that was within her revolted at the extinguishment of her last forlorn hope of home, of freedom. She grabbed the handle of the door and tugged at it futilely. It was locked, as were all the doors in the slave facility.

"Oh, god, please, not me, not me!' she shouted. "I won't go, you can't do this!"

The other girls were taken aback at Karen's gross breach of slave discipline. They grasped their fingers together tightly, their hands lodged behind their heads as if to give evidence of their non collusion with the rule breaker.

Madam Dupre had seen it before. Some of the girl's went docilely, some went tearfully and some tried to flee, to fight off the inevitable. But they all went. Dupre nodded at the guard who stood almost unnoticed in the corner during the colonel's selection. He walked calmly over to where Karen still yanked and tugged at the door handle as if by will she could overcome the locks and steel that held her in. The guard calmly removed his baton from his belt. Karen turned just in time to see him coming. Her mouth had just begun to form the word 'no' when the guard pressed the baton to her breast and unleashed a fierce jolt into her body. Karen's body stiffened and then collapsed. "Ohhhhhhh!' she cried as the pain flooded through her. The guard pushed the baton down between her splayed legs. She tried to push it away with her hands, but he was able to just press the tip between her upper thighs. 'Zap!' Another charge tore through Karen's body. Her legs shot out and her body lifted a half inch off of the floor. "Ahyaaaaaaaa!" she called out. She raised her hands. "No, no, please, no more, please!" she cried.

The guard stepped back. "Up!" was all he said.

Karen scrambled to her feet. Her face was awash with tears. Her mouth was set in a deep frown. "Please don't make me go, please!" she whined pitifully, looking at Madam Dupre, her rebellion quashed.

The guard had placed himself behind the distraught girl and, grabbing her arms, locked her wrists behind her. Karen's knees went weak and he held her up. Madam Dupre went over to a cabinet and retrieved a gag and a hood. The accouterments of bondage were never far away anywhere on Klitzman's island. As she approached the forlorn girl, Karen looked up and grimaced. She knew that she was done, that her fate was sealed. In a moment, she would be silenced. Her face grimaced in hatred. She looked Madam Dupre in the eye. "I hope you rot in hell!" she cried. It was the last thing she said. The smiling, ironic face of the slave mistress was the last thing she saw.

The colonel was ecstatic. He had truly made the best selection. The general would enjoy this girl's spirit. He would make her yell and scream. Her hatred was good. It would make her resistance a long and painful one, and her degradation ever so more enjoyable.

"With your permission, Colonel," Madam Dupre intoned, "I will have this slave made ready. If you wish, I will have her whipped."

"Oh, no, madam," the Asian answered, bowing slightly. "I enjoyed her display of spirit. I will tell the general and he will think of something appropriate."

"Very well," Dupre responded. She made a little brushing motion with her hand. The guard understood and took hold of Karen's arm with one meaty hand and dragged her to the door. After swiping his card and keying in his code, he opened it. His strong left hand practically lifted Karen from the ground and he marched her away. She would be taken directly upstairs and delivered to the transport hut. When the proper paperwork was completed, she would be prepared for transport and released to the colonel at his pleasure.

Dupre clapped her hands. "Ladies, back to your tasks," she instructed the four remaining, relieved slave girls.

The colonel cleared his throat. "If I may, Madam Dupre," he asked.

"Yes, colonel?" Dupre replied.

"If I may, I would appreciate the use of the dark eyed one, Mary I think is her name." He pointed. "Her."

Mary had been about to flee the room. She halted at Dupre's signal.

"Why, of course," the tall, slender slave mistress told the man. "Mary," she said, looking at the unhappy girl, "please go with the colonel." She turned back to the grinning Asian. "If she disappoints you in any way, colonel, please bring it to my attention and she will be severely punished. You may use room three, down on your left. There are whips and other confinements in the cabinets. Use her any way you wish. That's what she's here for."

Mary blanched at Madam Dupre's statement, "That's what she's here for." Well that was it, wasn't it? She was there to be used anyway anyone wished. But this was the first time anyone had said it so succinctly and so matter of factly. She looked at Col. Huong. A wave of fear swept through her. What would "anything" mean to him?

Huong made a short bow to Madam Dupre, joining his hands, palms together, just like you see in the movies. Politeness was the way of the East, but politeness that could cover a cruelty as harsh and as demonic as anything the West had to offer. The tall, thin, dark skinned man turned to Mary and made a similar expression of politeness. "You will follow me, please," he said.

Mary, naked and trembling, followed the Cambodian colonel down to the room that Madam Dupre had indicated. The room was a square of 20' width and length. Instead of a bed, there was a 10' x 10' cushioned, dark blue, cotton covered mat centered along one wall. The room was lit by several flower shaped sconces. Large, bright red, over stuffed pillows were strewn about and a light blue couch sat against the wall opposite the mat. The walls were covered by a dark brown, textured wallpaper, which, together with the dimmed light of the sconces, gave the spacious room a feeling of intimacy.

But what drew Mary's attention were the polished mahogany cabinet located against the far wall, the heavy chain dangling from the 8' high ceiling in the corner, the beringed ottoman and a strange wooden frame with a padded top. Her throat thickened as she contemplated what use the colonel would make of these objects or the things they contained.

Huong motioned for Mary to take a place on the mat. She obediently walked to the edge of the mat and removed her bright red high heels. She then stepped to the center of the mat and knelt, facing her 'client', as it were, as she had been taught, her legs spread, her hands palms up on her thighs.

A serving girl had followed them into the room. She carried a small tray and a menu. As was proper, she waited for the colonel to address her.

"Yes?" he said, casting an appreciative glance over her naked form.

"If it pleases the master," the short, blond haired, young girl said in a voice just louder than a whisper, "would you like to order any refreshments?"

Huong seemed to be pleasantly surprised by the suggestion.

"Yes," he responded. "Very much so."

The serving girl handed him the menu which he took several moments to examine. "Please bring me three large bottles of Perrier water, a small dish of cut limes and some ice," he said, not raising his eyes from the simple, cardboard carte du jour. "In one hour and a half you may bring me an order of the Cajun shrimp with rice. Please ask the chef to make it extra spicy." He looked up at the girl to ensure her comprehension of his request. She nodded at him and, with a bow, backed herself from the room. The steel door clanged shut, making Mary jump.

Huong stepped over to the couch, ignoring, for the moment, Mary's presence. He carefully undressed, and folded his clothes neatly on the chair. The young slave girl watched with fascination as the man began an almost ceremonial stretching of his muscles. She watched as she rocked his hips from side to side, his hands joined in an arch above his head. He did ten or fifteen, slow, carefully timed squats. His routine of exercises lasted about fifteen minutes. Mary could see a sheen of sweat on his body. As she watched his almost acrobatic movements, she pondered his instructions to the serving slave. One hour and a half, he said. Was he going to fuck her for an hour and a half?

Just as Huong had completed his preparations for his use of Mary's body, there was a buzzing at the door. Huong walked slowly over and opened it. The serving girl had brought his drink. She set the three green hued bottles on a small, round table near the door. She removed the bowl of ice and a small dish of cut limes from her tray and placed them down. She had brought only one glass.

Huong nodded politely to the slave who retreated wordlessly from the room. After placing some ice in the glass, using the ornate silver spoon the girl had left there, he twisted open a bottle and carefully and deliberately filled it with the sparkling water. He took up a wedge of lime and squeezed it into the glass. After stirring it slowly, he took up the glass and took a long, slow drink.

Everything that this man did was almost excruciatingly deliberate. Every movement seemed carefully choreographed. His firm, muscular body moved gracefully as if to some unheard song. When he finally placed the glass on the table and turned to look at the anxious, kneeling slave girl, Mary's heart sunk. Now it would come.

Huong walked onto the mat and knelt down on his haunches before the expectant girl. He closed his eyes, breathing deeply. After a few moments, he opened his eyes and peered deeply into Mary's. She was taken aback at the starkness of his stare. She tried to look away, but he raised his hands and placed them on either side of her head, forcing her gaze into his. The girl was awed by his prehensile strength. He placed his thumbs over her eyelids and brought her head towards his, forcing her to focus on his mesmerizing green eyes. Startled by the man's motion, Mary's body teetered forward. She instinctively placed her hand on the man's knee for balance. In a flash, Huong released his grip of her head and struck her face brutally with his outstretched palm. The powerful slap rang in Mary's ears. She uttered a surprised cry and fell to the mat. Her face burned where it had been struck. Huong looked at her with disdain. He poked his fingers into the mat in front of him forcefully. His meaning was clear, and the girl fearfully resumed her former position. Her eyes had filled with tears and her chest had begun to heave. When she had resumed her place, Huong waited for her reactions to subside. Although her body was trembling with apprehension, she gradually regained her breath. She fought back her tears and the burning sensation on her face faded.

After a few moments of pure silence, Huong again leaned forward and took Mary's head in his hands. He pulled her towards himself, again forcing her lids open with his thumbs. Mary was careful this time to maintain her balance. But the piercing stare of the colonel's eyes overwhelmed her and she darted her eyes side to side and up and down to avoid it. Huong slapped her face again, this time lightly, but the heavy mass of his hand reminded the girl of the consequences of disappointing the strange, demanding man.

The girl tried to keep her eyes focused on Huong's, but could not prevent her gaze from darting away. Each time, he gave her face another slap, each time a little harder. The man's silent strength was overpowering. Using all her will, and drawing on her fear of the man's precise and effective violence, Mary glued her gaze to his. She felt herself being drawn deeper and deeper into his spell. She understood that something strange and frightening was happening, that the man was sucking her will and her mind into his. If was if he was forcing a joinder of their souls, overpowering hers with his. She was startled, after many moments had passed, when the strange man, without breaking his gaze, began to push her gently back, so that she was lying flat on the mat.

When she was fully supine, he began to move his hands over her body. His gaze followed his firm, yet gentle hands. He carefully, deliberately, ran his hands down along her neck, over her shoulders and across her chest. His hands were strong and powerful and conveyed an electric charge each place they flowed. He slid them over and under her breasts, not caressing them, but feeling them, seemingly gaining a sense or knowledge of them.

When she had leaned back, Mary had drawn her arms down to her sides. Huong now grabbed her wrists and pulled her arms over her head, so they were outstretched on the mat above her. He dragged his hands down the length of her arms, feeling every muscle, every joint. Mary had closed her eyes and her mind followed the demanding, heat bearing hands on their journey of discovery.

Mary's consciousness followed Huong's hands as they descended her flanks and ran over her hips. He turned so that he faced towards her feet and, kneeling by her side, spread his touch over her taut belly and down the inside of her thighs. Mary expected him to seize her sex, which was aching with desire. The man's touch was enticing her body into lust. But he carefully brushed his hands lightly over her mons. His hands moved down her thighs, over her knees and down her shins to her feet. His hip nestled against Mary's side and she felt the heat of his body flowing into her.

When he had explored every inch of her feet, Huong carefully urged her body over, bringing her back and buttocks into the range of his electrifying hands. Mary's heart was pounding, although the man had not touched her sexually. She spread her thighs as his sensitive fingers moved up the back of her legs. He continued his upward exploration over the soft, white skin of her rear globes, drawing the cheeks apart, running his hand deliberately through the valley that ran between them. His hands rose up her back, over her shoulders and up her neck until her head was once more encased in his steel like grip.

Mary felt that her whole body was dangling in space, held up only by the firm hands on either side of her temples. Her skin tingled with an electric charge, ready to crackle into fire at the slightest movement. She wanted this man's body against hers, she craved it. He had captured her mind with his piercing, powerful stare and now had claimed every square inch of her body.

Suddenly, she felt him shifting his body over hers. He lay atop her back, covering her, achieving the maximum contact between his hot skin and hers. Mary sighed with passion. No one had ever touched her like this. Her body had never felt so alive, so sensitive to sensation. Maintaining bodily contact, he rolled her over so that she was again on her back. Again he pressed his body against hers, stretching his arms out to meet hers, pressing his chest against her bosom.

The slave girl groaned with lust as she felt his heat. But she felt that she dared not move, dared not break the spell he had put her under. He slid his torso off of hers and pulled her up until she was sitting in his lap. He circled his legs between hers and forced them open, locking his ankles over hers. He crossed his left hand across her breasts and pulled her sideways so that her hip lay against his groin. She was twisted in half, bent over. His legs and arm had her in an iron grip. She felt his free hand run down her back, caressing her hip. It then moved upwards until his hand was circled around the back of her neck. The man and the slave lay there still for a moment. Her body was imprisoned by his; she was utterly in his control. She felt his level, even breathing and fell into a dizzying trance.

It was then that she felt a slight pressure at the base of her neck. His thumb was gradually, but forcefully digging into her muscle. All at once a sharp stab of pain spread out from the point of contact. Mary drew in her breath in surprise. The pain was excruciating and she tried to shift her body or move her neck to avoid the pressure of Huong's digit. The man held her in his iron grip. The pain grew more and more intense as he pushed gradually harder and harder on the pressure point he had found. Mary's body jerked and convulsed with the pain. She cried out, "Ahhhhhhhhh! Oh, god, please stop, please!"

But the man did not stop. Mary screamed in pain and struggled desperately to free herself from his grasp. His strong arms kept hers pinned against his body. It was like he was inside her, controlling her every sensation, had captured her in a devious, immobilizing spell.

Huong let the slave girl cry and suffer for several minutes. He would withdraw the pressure slightly, giving the helpless woman's flesh and mind a moment's respite, and then again push hard against the nerve ending he had found, evoking another round of frantic screams and pleas.

For the next hour, Huong mercilessly tortured Mary's body. Rotating her body at will, keeping close contact between his skin and hers, his hands roamed her body as before, but using the knowledge he had gained as a roadmap to her most sensitive and vulnerable spots. He pushed his iron fingers into the interstices of her muscles, cramping them, drawing piteous moans of pain from the girl. He used his tightly muscled frame to extend her joints until she begged him to stop, pleading for mercy. He seemed to know the location of every nerve, every pressure point in her body, and used that knowledge to draw agonized screams of pain from the helpless girl. She felt as if her body was in the process of being digested by some fierce demon.

Huong had taken ownership of her mind and body in a very real sense. During the whole intense ordeal, his torso never lost contact with hers. She could feel his body's intense heat as he rolled her over and over, stopping only when he had chosen a new place to torment her. The only sounds in the room was her long drawn out moans of pain, her now feeble entreaties for him to stop, her piteous sobs.

Mary's mind was crazed with the almost continuous agonizing pain. Time dragged on slowly; every second of excruciating sensation seemed like it would last forever. She had been whipped brutally many times, but she had never experienced anything like this.

She found herself with her arms wedged tightly between his legs, her own legs splayed wide, his body wrapped around hers. Her muscles were tightly strained. His hand found her as yet ignored nether lips. The sudden contact with her sex startled her. She moaned with fear of what he would do to her there. Holding her tightly immobile, his fingers delicately pried them apart. She sensed herself lubricating as he gently stroked her slit. His prospective invasion of her inner self caused a wave of revulsion to flood over her. Moaning, her muscles still screaming in pain, she struggled futilely for release, for the power to refuse his caress. But he was too strong, too skilled for her to break his strangle hold. She cried and screamed, ranting her despair. When she felt his long, supple fingers enter her, felt them plunge deeply into her womb, she cried out, begging for respite, pleading for release.

As the cruel Asian worked her cunt, she felt her passion rising. She tried to fight it off, to deny him this dominion over her. But her body refused to obey her; her pussy moistened and expanded at the man's devilish touch. Her breathing became deeper, her legs began to involuntarily shudder.

Suddenly, she found herself twisted around. Her mind was too befogged with both pain and pleasure to comprehend how he did it, but she felt his stiff rod probe at the entrance to her sheath. Slowly, it crept inside her, pushing the walls aside, dragging itself over her electrified clit. Slowly, leisurely, the man stroked his iron-like rod inside her. Each stab of his prick deep into her womb pierced her very being. She shivered as she felt her lust begin to crest. She marshaled her forces for one last, futile attempt at freedom. Huong felt the desperateness of her move and tightened his control of her. "Ooooooooh!" she moaned as she felt her body succumb to the demands of her assailant's meaty staff. Her cunt clamped tightly around it. Her body convulsed as she came, wringing another long, woeful wail from her.

Her contractions subsided, but the man relentlessly continued his probing at her loins. "Noooooooo!' she called out as her blood began to rise again. "Noooooo, please, please!"

Huong's lust fed on Mary's pain and despair. He was on a plane of sensual delight far beyond Mary's understanding. He had carefully prepared his prey, had taken possession of her mind and body. He had driven all thought from her but the pain and pleasure he was inducing, all physical sensation except what he had imposed. Again and again, his cock still embedded deeply within her, between rounds of exquisite pain, he made her come. Finally, he felt it was time to enjoy release. He would let his mind float in a sea of pleasure. He eased his firm mastery of his own responses, letting his lust carry him away. As his cock exploded, he felt the twin forces of life and death flow through him. He squeezed Mary tightly as he felt her crisis begin anew, bringing her to new heights of pain and pleasure all at once. She moaned and cried as she came.

When his cock had ceased its spasms, he allowed his body to relax. Mary felt his grip on her loosen. He released her and she rolled to the mat, her body limp. She gave great thanks for her release. She could not control herself and began to sob heavily. Huong closed his eyes and sat back on his haunches, the very position he had adopted before the beginning of his cunning and ruthless assault of the young slave girl. He drank in Mary's pain with his ears.

The Cambodian colonel was sitting entranced when there was a timid knocking on the door. He rose and opened it, admitting the serving slave. She had brought his repast and placed the steaming plate down on the table. He thanked her and ushered her out the door.

Before consuming his meal, Huong made a trip to the dark mahogany cabinet on the other side of the room. Mary was oblivious to his actions, grateful to have a surcease of her ordeal.

Huong returned to the mat. Mary felt his hands on her ankle. He drew her left leg up and connected to the leather bracelet surrounding her right wrist. Mary had no strength to resist. She docilely permitted him to connect the bracelet on her right ankle to the one on her left wrist. He pulled her to her knees and turned her torso so that she was facing the door. Mary looked at the man forlornly. She knew that the cruel man had not done with her. Her knees were spread open and her ankles and wrists were crisscrossed behind her.

Huong moved behind Mary and he drew a black blindfold across her eyes, tying it off behind her head, plunging the girl into darkness. She cringed in expectation of further torment. She felt a pressure on her mouth, and a large ring gag was forced in between her teeth. There was a sharp pain in her breasts as Huong applied a sharp toothed clamp to each nipple. Mary winced at the pain, emitting a strange sounding moan through her forced open mouth.

Huong's hand descended to her loins and, pinching her tender labia, placed a long, thick clamp over them. The tight spring of the clamp pressed her cunt lips together tightly. She issued a half moan, half cry.

Satisfied that the girl's experience of pain and isolation would occupy her, Huong settled down to his meal. He sat cross legged at the table, facing his victim. He watched her carefully as he ate.

Mary fought back her tears and moans as she listened to the colonel consume his dinner. She could hear the feint tap of his chop sticks as he fed himself his shrimp and rice. She listened as he poured himself another glass of soda water, hearing the clink of the ice, the gentle fizzing of the liquid.

It seemed to Mary hours before she heard he man rise. Her nipples felt like they were on fire. Her poor labia ached and burned. She heard him walk back to the cabinet, and she shivered in apprehension as she speculated as to what implement of torture he would produce next. She sensed him kneeling down before her. His hand passed between her legs and removed the painful clamp that had captured her pussy's lips. Her loins stung fiercely as blood ran back into her tortured nether lips.

Huong considered the delicately beautiful creature before him. He would have picked her, had he been picking for himself. She had proven an immeasurable delight. He reached out to her pink, round breasts and removed the clamps from her nipples. Mary whined involuntarily from the pain of their release. He placed his hands on the firm, youthful mounds and caressed them. His touch was gentle, almost soothing. Mary's nipples stiffened in reaction to the stimulation of her breasts.

The slave girl knew what a ring gag was for, and she was anticipating the man's imminent callous use of her mouth. She wanted this ordeal to be over. She yearned for the relative safety of the slave dorm. Her whole body seemed to be in pain. Her mind rebelled in protest against her abuse.

Huong's hand descended to Mary's tender slit. As before, he expertly manipulated her to moistness. He rubbed her pleasure bud, tickling and pulling at it until the sheath below opened to his fingers. He watched Mary's face as he gradually brought on her lust. When she had begun to pant, her breasts swollen with her hot blood, he stood up and walked behind her. His cock had hardened as he had watched Mary's passion rise and he was ready to encase it in her widespread mouth.

Pulling the girl's head back by her hair, he forced her back to arch so that her mouth was poised for penetration by his prick. He grabbed her chin with one hand and slowly pushed his cock past her strained lips, deep into her mouth. Mary felt his hot meat press against her tongue and its tip pass into her throat.

For a moment, Huong paused, his one hand holding Mary's chin tightly, letting the tight confines of Mary's esophagus inflame his passion. He had a tasseled whip in the other. He raised his arm and brought it down harshly on the blindfolded girl's cunt.

Mary was shocked by the violent explosion of pain in her loins. She screamed and yelled as it coursed through her. The vibrations of Mary's throat sent a jolt of intense pleasure through Huong's encased meat. He closed his eyes and enjoyed the product of his cruelty. When he sensed that Mary had begun to choke and gag desperately for air, he slowly withdrew his tool until she was able to draw an agonized breath. When she had refilled her lungs with air, he slowly and deliberately pushed his meat back down into her, and, when it was embedded, struck the helpless girl again with the whip.

Mary struggled and screamed each time the whip bit at her loins. Each time, the vibrations of her throat sent a wave of pleasure flowed through Huong's manhood. Each time, he withdrew it only when Mary's chest began to heave in protest at the lack of oxygen. Finally, his lust rising, his blood boiling, he shoved his cock deeply into Mary's tortured throat and spilled his hot seed inside.

He was sated. The slave girl had given him much pleasure. He released her head and let her fall gently to her side. Rolling her to her stomach, he released her wrists and ankles and then rejoined them, wrist to wrist, ankle to ankle. He walked to the cabinet and returned with a thick, leather plug. After removing the ring gag from the sobbing girl's mouth, he pushed the thick wad of leather inside and buckled the gag behind her head.

He walked to the couch and slowly and deliberately dressed. When he was done, he walked back onto the mat and knelt down to the helpless, supine girl. He placed his mouth by her ear and whispered to her softly.

"Soon, I will be very rich. When that happens, I will return here to claim you and bring you home with me."

He rose, paused to appreciate the delightful flesh of the dismal girl, and left.

CHAPTER TEN
LANA GOES DANCING

Mary spent the next few days recovering from her ordeal in the infirmary. As soon as Col. Huong had left, she was rescued by her slave supervisor, Giselle. The use of slave girls throughout Klitzman's resort was carefully monitored, especially with new guests. Drunken fisted brutality was not tolerated. Each girl represented an investment and broken bones, smashed faces and other disfigurements were not generally allowed. There were exceptions, of course, but only for special guests. And so Huong's torture of the young girl was observed by a concealed video camera. Giselle was aware that Mary would be in need of some assistance before Hung had even left.

The girl could hardly move when Giselle released her from her bonds. Giselle asked, very politely, one of the guards to carry Mary to the infirmary where her muscles were quickly iced down to inhibit swelling and she was given a muscle relaxant. But nothing could dispel Mary's frantic fear of Huong's eventual return.

It was time for the other girls from that fateful plane trip to take their places within the resort. Lana had been selected for something special. She had never thought of herself as beautiful or sultry, but many women underestimate their charms, and Lana was one of them. She had thinned out some as a result of her training regimen, and the exercise had helped tone an already graceful, desirable form.

Madam Dupre was always on the lookout for those special girls who could serve in the so called 'lounges' of the resort. The men who came here expected a sexually liberating experience and ready access to beautiful, willing young women. But they needed some entertainment too. The lounges served to provide some distraction for the guests. There was a jazz club, where tapes of modern and classical jazz was mixed with live performances by women who had been especially recruited for that purpose. They were slave girls, naturally, and they were available, when off duty, for the guests' amusement.

The resort also had a strip club, a rock and roll club, no headbanger music allowed, and a disco. The women who worked these clubs were dressed in provocative fashions, appropriate for the club's ambiance, and were available to be 'picked up' as it were, by the gentlemen who visited there. Supervisors, men who were either directly employed by the resort, or men who had positions of trust in one or the other of Klitzman's many worldwide endeavors, were discouraged from picking up girls in the clubs, except when they were in the process of entertaining a guest. Those girls were made available to the supervisors by special arrangement, however.

But the lounges were principally designed for the guests. Guests were either men of great power and political influence or men of vast wealth who could afford the resort's steep fees. All of the men who came as guests were carefully vetted before membership was proffered. And they were sworn to absolute secrecy, a pledge secured by their very lives and the lives of those around them. It was easy to discern the guests from the supervisors. Guests wore soft, cotton robes of pastel blue. Supervisors wore similar robes of reddish brown. No personal clothing was permitted in the main resort compound, no personal property, no cash, no identification, no cell phones, no jewelry. Everything was checked at the gate. And if the robes were somewhat off-putting to guests or supervisors when they first arrived, they soon got used to them because everyone was wearing one. Even the guards, who wore robes dyed coal black.

Dupre had Lana's background material, and much was known of her prior life. When recruited by the man she knew as Paderovski for the modeling scam, Lana had answered an extensive questionnaire about her life. Dancing had been high on her list of favorite activities.

And so when Lana entered Madam Dupre's suite on the instructions of Giselle, her female supervisor, strictly distinguishable from the male supervisors in both rights and authority, the manager of the disco lounge was sitting in a comfortable, padded chair adjacent to Dupre's regency styled couch. Dupre was behind her desk.

When Lana had learned of her summons to Madam Dupre's chambers, she had quailed in fear. The slave mistress was well known for her cruelty and often girls who were summoned there were never seen again. But she steeled her nerves and entered the office prepared for the worst.

The naked, black haired Latina stepped to the taped line that she had stood at the first day she had been brought down to the slave facility a little more than ten days ago. She placed her hands behind her head and spread her legs.

Madam Dupre looked up at the slave girl. She was very attractive, and the training had done her good. Her plump breasts sat invitingly high on her chest. Her stomach was flat and tight. There was a trace of short, black hair surrounding her nether lips.

"Well, Cholo," she said to the lean, light brown skinned man sitting on the chair, "what do you think?"

Lana was surprised at Madam Dupre's statement since she had not seen anyone else in the room when she entered. She dared not turn to see who the slave mistress was talking to.

"From where I sit," the wiry man replied, "she looks pretty good."

"Lana, please turn around for Master Cholo," Dupre instructed her.

The slave girl turned her body around without moving her hands from behind her head. The lighting in Madam Dupre's office was soft, but good. She saw the man who Dupre had spoken to. Her heart skipped. He was mean looking, with a broad scar across the right side of his face, obscured slightly by a rough, black beard. He had piercing eyes and a tight, thin lipped mouth. His jet black hair was carefully styled. He was wearing the reddish brown robe of a supervisor.

"She has excellent tits," he said as his eyes glossed over Lana's form. "Come here," he ordered the girl.

Lana fearfully stepped closer to the man. She stopped when her knees were almost touching his. He leaned forward in his chair and placed his hands on Lana's hips. His eyes carefully examined her flesh. He tested the firmness of her thighs and the flatness of her stomach. He motioned for her to lean over and placed his hands on her quivering breasts. Lana knew that she was being measured, but for what? Should she hope to please this cruel looking man, or should she pray that he rejected her? She gasped slightly when Cholo pinched her thick, prominent nipples.

"Looks good," Cholo said, almost to himself. He moved a hand between her thighs and grabbed her labia between his thumb and forefinger. When he squeezed them tightly, Lana winced with pain, a reaction that Cholo closely observed since, as she was still leaning over, her breasts floating free from her body, her face was inches from his. She felt the man's hand begin to stroke her sex. Cholo was watching her face carefully as he looked for signs of nascent passion.

Lana had always been a passionate girl. Manuelo had not been her first lover. She had lost her virginity at fifteen to a lanky, dark skinned Cuban boy. Sex had been an important part of her life ever since, although she had been careful not to develop a reputation as a whore or an easy lay. She usually stuck with one partner for several months or more and was always careful to use protection. Since her arrival at Klitzman's island, her sexuality had blossomed although she had not developed the obsessive craving for it as had Sheila. When the fucking was good, her body enjoyed it, even as her mind rebelled against it.

As Cholo continued to caress her moistened slit and her little bud of pleasure, it was not long before Lana's cunt was oozing lubrication and her plush nether lips had engorged. Cholo was gently rubbing her hardened clit when she gave out a little sigh of incipient lust. Her face had reflected her growing physical desire, and Cholo had noticed it.

He withdrew his hand and waived Lana away. "I'll give her a try," he told Dupre. "I'll take her over to the club now and give her a workout."

Lana had heard of the clubs from the other slave girls. The girls who worked them as waitresses resided in the slave dorm. They had talked about the beautiful dresses that the 'lounge girls' wore. And the lounge girls had their own dormitory and got special privileges. If she had to serve as a slave, that sounded better than the other slave duties that had been described to her. But what about this harsh looking man? Would he beat her? He would certainly fuck her.

Cholo gut up from the chair. "If you have a gag, I'll take her up now."

Madam Dupre pressed the intercom on her desk. A female voice answered. "Yes, mistress."

"Bring me a travel gag."

"Yes, mistress," the girl answered.

Moments later, Madam Dupre's short, pixie-like secretary entered the room. Her tiny breasts were connected by a silver chain. The ends of the chain were connected to delicate silver rings through her nipples. Hanging in the middle of the chain was a small black disc, bearing the emblem of the resort, the cursive, red '*k*'. She carried a thick leather gag connected to a leather shield that covered the whole lower face and the jaw, and a strap to be buckled behind the head. She handed it to Cholo who inserted the gag into Lana's docile mouth. He pulled the belt tight forcing the leather plug in deeply. The lower half of her face was now concealed and confined.

Cholo had a four foot long steel chain leash in the pocket of his robe. It had a bright red leather handle. He connected the leash to Lana's collar and pulled her from the room.

Lana realized that she was now in the custody of this unknown man. She had not been fucked since she had been released from Rukimo's dungeon, but she expected she would be soon. She scurried behind the swift walking man, careful to maintain her balance on her bright red, high heel shoes.

Once Cholo had brought her upstairs on the elevator, he led her down one of the red brick paths. Lana was unused to the tropical heat and she began to sweat as she was hurried along. She could hear the click of her heels on the red brick pathway. She stared at the seemingly numberless naked and gagged women moving quickly around them. The men she saw walked leisurely, smiling and joking with one another. It was strange to be trotting among them, her breasts jolting with each hurried step, with nary a glance at her naked form.

The outside of the disco club looked like any other that you might find in New York, Miami or Los Angeles. It had a dark green canopy over the entrance and a set of neon lights overhead that announced "The Inferno". It was about 11 A.M. and the club was empty except for two of the native servants who were restocking the bars. There were two large semi-circular bars on each side of the room. The ceiling was mirrored and the walls were painted black. The dance floor was in between the bars and had light fixtures set in the tile. It was well air-conditioned, as were all of the resort buildings. Cholo led Lana towards the far side of the room. There was a stairway going up and down. Cholo took the down stairs. Lana almost fell as she tried to keep up with his pace on the stairs. The downstairs held the storage rooms for the liquor stock, a huge cooler for beer, Cholo's office and a large dance studio. It had a shiny hard maple floor, a mirror along one wall and two loudspeakers mounted from the ceiling. There were several cages along one wall and a forlorn looking young woman was locked in one of them.

Cholo looked at the gagged and bound woman in the cage. There was a telephone on the wall next to the door and he picked it up and dialed.

After a moment, he spoke. "Yeah, this is Cholo. I thought I told you to get this cunt out of here....Yeah.....Yeah....Well I want her out before three this afternoon. The other girls have to warm up and I don't want this bitch here when they arrive, got it?" He slammed down the phone. The girl in the cage just cringed.

Lana was unhooked from the leash and her wrists were unbound. Cholo left her standing there while he walked through a doorway on the far side of the room. The doorway was built right into the mirrored wall. A moment later he reemerged. He was carrying a delicate, coffee colored dress, with rhinestones and sparkles strewn over it.

"You're about a size two, aren't you?" he asked the girl.

Lana was surprised to be asked anything. She was still gagged and so she could only answer the man with a nod.

"Then put this on. What's your shoe size?"

Lana answered by holding up six fingers.

Cholo went back through the door. Lana was ecstatic at the opportunity to wear clothes and quickly had the dress up over her head and down her hips. It was a little tight up front, but fit her shoulders nicely. The bodice was cut deep and her nipples rested just below the neckline. The skirt was cut away to the left and it draped diagonally to just below her left knee. She looked at herself in the mirror and swirled slowly around, letting the skirt billow out. If it weren't for the stark leather shield over the lower half of her face, and the thick leather collar and bracelets, she would look lovely. She ran her hands down her hips, reveling in the touch of the soft fabric against her body.

When Cholo returned he had three shoeboxes. "Here's a 5 ½, a 6 and a 6 ½. See which one fits best." He instructed her. He watched her intently as she doffed her bright red high heels and donned a pair of the black patent leather shoes. They hard sharp pointy toes and medium sized heels. The spikes had broad bases to facilitate dancing. The 6 ½'s fit perfectly.

"Wait here," Cholo said as he picked up the shoe boxes and went back through the mirrored door. He returned quickly and walked to a small recess in the wall on the right side of the room. Lana heard the loud, beating rhythm of a salsa beat. She recognized the song. It had been a hit a year or so ago. It was a favorite. She fought off the memories of happy times that the song brought. She had an audition to perform.

Cholo walked over to the girl. "Let's see you move," he ordered.

Lana found it hard to believe that she would have to audition with her gag still in place. Dancing was physically demanding, at least this type, and she worried about being able to draw deep enough breaths through her nose. Frightened, nervous, she began to dance in time with the music. She hoped that her body would remember her salsa moves.

"No! No!" Cholo yelled. "Not like that. I didn't say dance. I said move. Sway your hips; let me see if you're an *ignara puta* or a Latina princess."

Lana let the insult roll off of her. She would show this *cholero* what a full blooded real Latina could do. Lana looked down at her feet. She tried to block out all that had happened to her and her friends since they had stepped off the plane when they arrived at Klitzman's island. She tried to forget the weeks of torment she had suffered and that this street thug, this serial rapist, was going to judge her as to whether she was suitable to fuck his customers. She let the rhythm of the music flow through her. She began to tap her toe.

The black haired slave girl began to sway her hips slowly. She closed her eyes and let the music enter her. All else was gone. Just the sensuous, love song remained. Once the music took over, she began to move her upper body. She felt her breasts gently swaying as she moved, her hair begin to swirl in the air. She could have been anyplace, anyplace in the world. Her mind felt liberated, free.

Cholo stepped forwards and grabbed her swinging arms. She opened her eyes at the sudden movement, and then they were off. Cholo led her through the dance steps like a master. His body breathed sensuality. Lana felt that she was on air as she became who she once was, a happy, liberated, proud, Latina. The singer cried out his agony over his lost love in deep, smooth, plaintive tones. For the moment, Lana was that lost love. She had a lover who pined for her, who called her *mi corazón*.

All of Lana's energy was poured into the dance. She knew that, in a way, she was dancing for her life. To be able to dance would be a wondrous gift after all she had gone through. She danced like she never had before.

When the song ended, Lana was huffing and puffing. She had strained to keep dancing even though her heart was pumping madly, straining for oxygen. Towards the end, limited by what breath she could bring in through her nose, she had begun to feel dizzy. Now, she tried to recover her breath so that she could receive the verdict of this callous man.

"Okay," he said. "I'll give you a try." He was breathing heavy too, a sign that he had been excited by his turn on the floor with the girl. "Okay," he repeated, "take off the dress and the shoes."

Lana hurried to obey her overlord. Careful not to tear the fine silken material, she grabbed the hem of the skirt and lifted it over her head. She was a naked slave once more. She handed it to Cholo who tossed it on the floor. "The shoes," was all he said.

Lana stepped out of the shiny, black shoes and placed them aside.

"Clam position," Cholo ordered.

The slave girls had been taught a series of simple commands. Rather than have to describe at length a special posture or position the master desired from the slave girl, he could utter a one word command and the girl would know what to do. 'Clam' denoted kneeling on the floor, legs slightly apart, crouched over with the breasts crushed against the knees, elbows on the floor, head down. It was a simulation of a closed shellfish. 'Swan', 'dog', 'snake', 'frog', were all commands denoting a specific position. 'Ostrich' was similar to 'clam' but the slave's head would be forward, legs spread wider, arms out beside the head and forehead on the floor, like an ostrich with its head in a hole.

Lana dropped to the floor and adopted the 'clam' position. As she assumed it was a prelude to her use, she turned first so that her haunches would be presented to her master. In this position, only one orifice was conveniently available. Lana knew this and began to relax, as best she could, the muscles that governed her rear entrance. Out of the corner of her eye, she saw Cholo's brown robe tossed to the floor. She felt him kneel behind her. He placed his hands on her arched back and caressed her soft skin. He ran them down to her inviting buttocks. Cholo was not a man to waste time in extended foreplay. His cock was hard and it needed a warm, moist place. He preferred the tight ring of the rear entrance to the lush, moist sheath. And he had no interest in giving women pleasure.

Lana felt Cholo's hard meat press against the opening of her rear passage. Even though she had tried to loosen the ring of flesh to permit the easy entrance of a hot, thick member, Cholo's cock pressed on the edges of Lana's brown star, stretching them. Lana suppressed a cry of pain. She was grateful when she felt the entrance to her bowels loosen and Cholo's member slide in.

She had never permitted any man this privilege before her abduction and enslavement. She had had to work hard to overcome her revulsion as the strong African men in Rukimo's dungeon forced it on her. She had cried and screamed in pain and humiliation. But she had learned to tolerate it, and then to even derive some pleasure from it. As Cholo's cock dragged back and forth against the pursed opening of her bowels, Lana closed her eyes and let the sensation of his shaft against her sensitive flesh run through her. Following her training, the slave girl timed the tightening of her rear entrance with the backwards stroke of Cholo's cock. He moaned on his withdrawal, and, further energized by the intense pleasure of the tight ring around his shaft, plunged his dick forwards again, burying it to its hilt.

Cholo's grunts as he plowed Lana's ass echoed through the room. The girl broke position and looked up seeing her reflection in the mirror. Her body was crouched down as if closely bound. Cholo's sweaty torso rose from behind her, his face tense with growing passion, his eyes closed, his head tilted back. The man's breathing was getting harder and harder. Lana saw his face become red, his eyes squeeze shut. Her own lusts were rising, excited by the vision of this stranger plowing her rear. When she felt Cholo's cock throb and pulse within her, she was shocked to find that she her own lusts had crested. At each pump of Cholo's hot sperm into her bowels, her cunt pulsed with pleasure. She moaned as she came. She looked again in the mirror and saw her face as she had never seen it: lustful, hungry for a man's cock.

When Cholo's forces were exhausted, his flaccid cock slid from Lana's rear. He got to his feet and, without a word to the kneeling girl walked off. He went through the mirrored door and returned about thirty seconds later drying his cock with a paper towel. She saw that he also had a whip in his hand.

Lana's heart began to thump in her chest at the thought of the pain to come. All remnants of her recent pleasure fled from her mind. As Cholo walked behind her, she closed her eyes and steeled herself for the blows. She heard her master's voice.

"This is just a taste of what faces you if you should disappoint me," he told the frightened young woman. "Just a taste."

Cholo landed five hard strokes of a rattan cane across Lana's rear globes. She cried out in pain at each one. They felt like strips of fire running across her skin. "Ohhhhh!" she cried as each one landed. She had struggled not to cry, but the tears came all of themselves, washing down her florid cheeks. Her cries resounded off of the bare walls of the room, reverberating in her mind. When the man was done, Lana looked up in the mirror to see her red rimmed eyes, her tear stained face. She met Cholo's eyes there. He smiled at her.

"When I get to know you better, I'll take you back to my place and teach you what pain is really like. That okay with you, *comerita*?"

Lana, unable to speak, nodded her head in reluctant affirmation. She watched him in the mirror as he picked up the dress and shoes.

"I'll be back for you later, *crica*," he told her. He took the materials back behind the mirrored wall. Lana looked up at him as he came back.

"Keep your head down, *puta!*" he ordered. Lana lowered her eyes to the floor.

She remained in that position for what seemed like hours. Time dragged on unmercifully slowly. She could hear the woman in the corner shifting about in her cage. There no other sounds except for her breathing. She was too frightened to move even an inch, although her muscles had begun to cramp painfully. She could feel her plump breasts crushed against her knees, Cholo's discharge leaking from her rear. Her buttocks burned from her beating. She just kept repeating to herself that life would be better here. In spite of the bandit's threats, she would be able to dance, to feel freedom even if for a short while. She would do anything to stay.

Kneeling inside a tiny space in the middle of a vast room made Lena appreciate what a small cog she was in a huge machine. She imagined how she looked, a naked, kneeling woman, all drawn up as if inside a cage, her compressed figure reflected in the mirror that she could not see, her body a mound of light brown flesh amidst the yellowish brown polished wood. But she was in a cage, a cage not of steel, but of words. Cholo's command to remain as he had left her was as strong a bond as steel chains. She felt puny and powerless. She had no real idea where she was, never mind having any ideas about escape. She would just have to pray that someday, somehow, someone would come to save her.

Lana heard the door behind her open. Footsteps sounded on the hardwood floor. She sensed a male presence. Had Cholo come to free her, she wondered. Then she heard a voice speak, a coarse, cruel voice. It was not Cholo's.

"Get up, cunt," the voice said. Lana quickly rose to her feet, ignoring the painful cramps in her thighs and back. She felt hands locking her wrists together behind her. A black bag was drawn over her head. Hands turned her body around. A leash attached to her collar. She felt herself being tugged forwards.

"What is happening?" she thought to herself urgently. "Where is this man taking me?" Could it be that Cholo had changed his mind? No, she realized. It was a mistake. They were supposed to come for the other girl. They were taking her away instead. Lana's hope for a happier life evaporated. "Oh, god!" she thought. "What will happen to me now?"

She could not protest or explain since she still bore the gag that Cholo had installed earlier that day. Even if Cholo were in the bar upstairs, she was hooded and she doubted that he would recognize her by the shape of her body alone. As she was pulled up the stairs, she cried and moaned.

"Shut the fuck up!" the man who was taking her away said. "I'll tell them to beat you when we get to the boat."

"Boat?" Lana thought, panicked. She was being sent away somewhere! If Cholo had intended to send the woman downstairs away as a punishment, wherever she was going had to be much worse than whatever fate could hold for her in the resort. She started to pull back on her leash. She fell to the floor so that the man would have to drag her from the club. She kicked and screamed from behind her gag. A fist landed solidly on her thigh. The pain was excruciating. She heard a familiar voice.

"What the fuck is the matter with you? Can't you handle a simple job like this?" It was Cholo and he was yelling at the man for losing control of his prisoner. "Get her the fuck out of my bar!" he yelled.

The man grabbed Lana by the ring in her collar and lifted her into the air. She squirmed and cried out as he dragged her to the door. At the last moment, Cholo looked around to watch them exit. He saw the five deep, red lines across Lana's rear.

"Hold it! Hold it!" he yelled. "Get that cunt back in here!"

Lana felt her body being turned around and moved towards Cholo's voice.

"Get that bag off of her head!" Cholo ordered.

Lana felt the bag being removed. When her sight was restored, she saw the angry, red face of her 'employer'.

"That's not the one, asshole!" Cholo yelled at the man.

"What do you mean?" the man asked.

"Didn't you check her number? It's the one in the cage, stupid!"

"I didn't see anyone in a cage," the man replied.

"Did you look?" Cholo asked, his voice full of irritation. He waited for an answer. None came. "I didn't think so," Cholo said. "This one just came in today. Why the fuck would I be sending her to the mainland? Eh?" Cholo was barely containing his anger. Being sent to the mainland meant being turned over to one of the native whorehouses, where life was ugly, brutish and short.

While he was at Klitzman's island, Cholo helped out by running the disco club. It gave him something to do. He could play big shot with the guests. But most of the time, he was a stone cold killer.

There was a very pregnant pause. Lana looked at Cholo with undiluted relief. After a moment, Cholo seemed to get hold of himself. In a tense, but calm voice, he instructed the man carefully. "Let this cunt go. Go downstairs and get the other cunt. And then get you and her out of my club. *Comprende?*"

"Yes, sir," the man said meekly. Lana was released from the leash and the man went downstairs. In a few moments he returned with another naked and bound, hooded woman. She followed him docilely out the door.

Later that afternoon, Lana finally had her gag removed. The other dancers for the club, fourteen of them in all, arrived at 3 p.m. They had been led around the perimeter of the resort compound in a coffle, naked and bound. It would spoil the illusion of the club for the guests to see them in their servile state. Once inside the club, they were led to a sort of lounge cum dressing room in the basement, one floor below the dancing studio. The rule of silence did not pertain there and they were soon chatting noisily. Lana had been left there, standing alone in the room since her brush with exile to the mainland. The guard that released the other dancers unbound her wrists from behind her back and removed her gag. A tall woman, with long chestnut colored hair approached her. She was a little older than the rest of the girls, maybe 25 or 26. She gave Lana a hug.

"My name is Yolanda," she said. "I'm the mother hen of this little group. What's your name?"

Lana's jaw ached from its long confinement and it took her a moment to answer.

"I'm happy to meet you, Lana. I know that this is all very strange to you, but it's not too bad, really. I assume that you have met Cholo."

Lana nodded. She was still too taken aback by being surrounded by what seemed to be a gaggle of normal, happy, young women to give more than perfunctory responses.

"He's not here much," Yolanda told her, holding Lana's hand in hers. "And he pretty much leaves us alone. Danny really runs the club and he's much nicer. But let me introduce you to the girls. I won't say their names, you'll learn them eventually, but it's too much to get all at once."

She turned to the chattering young women. "Girls," she shouted over the din. "This is Lana. She's the new dancer. Please make her feel welcome."

The young women called out various greetings to Lana. She noticed that they were not wearing the standard leather collars and bracelets of the club. Their bindings were made of dark brown, polished leather. The rings were made of a gold alloy, gold by itself being too likely to chip and bend. They were all pretty with lithe bodies and beautiful, shapely breasts. There were no ugly or plain women on Klitzman's island, but these girls were a cut above the rest.

While they were chatting, the girls had been donning tight fitting leotards and leg warmers. Yolanda showed Lana where her dressing station was and found her a leotard that fit.

"We'll be going upstairs for some workouts and dancing in a few moments. After about an hour or so of practice, we'll come back for dinner. Then we'll dress for work. I'll find you something really pretty to wear." Yolanda's smile was comforting to Lana. She had been afraid that she would be shunned since she was replacing a girl who was probably a friend to most of these young women. She mentioned her concern to Yolanda

"Oh, please don't think that, Lana. We all know it's not your fault. These things happen. Someday we'll all be shipped out to somewhere or other. We try not to think about it."

"But what happened?" Lana asked.

"I'm afraid that Linda got into a conflict with a guest. He was going to burn her with a cigarette and she slapped him."

"Oh!" Lana said, shocked at both the action of the guest and the girl's response.

"She knew better," Yolanda said. "The guest would probably have had his privileges suspended. They can beat us, but they can't scar us. Anyway, we have no right to disobey any order of a guest or supervisor, never mind strike one."

Yolanda put her arm around the black haired girl. "I've been here for five years. I've seen many slave girls come and go. Smile, obey and fuck like a bunny. That's all the protection you have against being punished. It's not a guarantee, but as a rule it will keep the whippings to a tolerable level. The guests don't usually come to the club to find a girl to whip. They want to dance, have fun, get blown. Occasionally, one will come in looking for a beautiful girl to abuse, but not often."

Lana listened to the older woman with her full attention. Anything anyone could tell her to help her avoid pain was very welcomed.

"Now get dressed, Lana. We'll be going upstairs in a few minutes.

The workout was long and hard. Lana felt her muscles turn to rubber. One of the girls, a pretty Jewish girl from Staten Island, showed her some new steps. When they were finished their routines, they all went back downstairs, in the company of a guard of course, and showered. They would change after they had time to rest and eat.

The girls all lay down on cots to take short naps. Lana dozed off and was awoken by one of the girls so that she could eat. Dinner was sent down on a dumbwaiter. It was light, consisting of some cheese, salad and fruit. By the time they had finished eating, it was about 6 o'clock. The club opened officially at 8 and the girls had to be ready by 7:30. They sat at their dressing stations and carefully applied makeup. Yolanda made sure that Lana was properly instructed in what to do.

Each girl had a set of almost scandalously revealing dresses. Yolanda found one that fit Lana. "You'll probably be measured tomorrow. It'll take a few days for them to set you up. In the meantime, find a couple of girls your size. They'll let you borrow. I'll have one of the guards come down and change your collar and bracelets."

The girl's dressed quickly, yet deliberately. Girls whose décor was not perfect faced discipline. Too many times and you were out.

The dress that Yolanda chose for Lana was bright red. The skirt was made of several layers of light translucent chiffon, barely concealing her legs and the apex of her thighs. It had thin shoulder straps holding up a bodice that revealed most of her breasts. The bodice fit tightly over her chest. "The men will love to watch your tits move in that," Yolanda told her. "Don't forget why we're here. As distasteful as it may seem, it's your job to make the men want to fuck you. We have a saying. If you don't get fucked, you're fucked." Yolanda gave a little laugh.

Lana was thrilled to adorn herself with sheer black stockings. The silky feel of the nylons was comforting. She tested a few perfumes and selected one that suited her tastes. She painted her lips a bright red to match her dress. One of the girls, a dark skinned, luscious looking, Brazilian girl with wild black curls gave her a pair of globe shaped, gold earrings.

"Don't lose them, *pettita*, or I'll scratch your eyes out," she said, only half joking.

At 7:15, the girls were all ready. They were all gorgeously outfitted. They checked themselves out in the floor length mirrors. Lana could see why Yolanda had lasted so long. She was graceful and elegant. She had on a yellow shift dress with slits up both sides. It clung to her hips tightly and displayed her long, sultry legs to good effect. All of the girls wore low heeled shoes, colored to match their dresses.

At 7:25, the door to the dressing room opened. A heavy set, bearded man stepped in the room. He was wearing a reddish brown robe. "Everybody ready, ladies?" he asked. His voice was deep with a decidedly American accent. There was a general murmur of assent. "Where's the new girl?" he asked.

Lana stepped forwards cautiously. "Here I am, master," she said.

"None of that 'master' stuff while you're in the club. Except for Cholo, of course. You better make sure you're real nice to him." The man looked around at the milling crowd of exquisite pulchritude. "The rest of you girls go upstairs. I want to talk to Lana."

The girls shuffled out quietly. Outside of the dressing room, and until and unless they were entertaining a guest, all the rules of the resort applied. When the door closed, the man sat on a chair and beckoned Lana to approach him.

"Let me see, honey. Turn around," he instructed her.

Lana did a little pirouette. The skirt swirled nicely around her. Her black stockings, held up by pretty, flowered garters, accentuated the area that they didn't cover. The light brown skin of her upper thighs and her available love lips were readily discernable.

"Nice, nice. By the way, my name is Danny. If you're lucky, you'll be dealing mostly with me. I try to be fair and I have no need to throw my weight around, if you'll pardon the pun." Lana managed a weak smile.

"That's my girl," he said. "Come and sit on my lap."

Lana obeyed the man's order and perched herself on his rotund, but muscular thigh. He took the hem of Lana's skirt and brazenly pushed it up around her waist. Lana was embarrassed at the nakedness of her loins. The act of dressing up had made her momentarily forget that any man on the island had the right to see her naked anytime that they wanted. Having her skirt lifted so casually brought her status as a slave quickly back into focus.

Danny ran his fat hand over her thighs. "Very pretty, Lana. And a pretty little cunt. Make sure you get it stuffed tonight, all right?"

Lana nodded obediently.

He stroked her labia with his fingers. "You'll have to show me your skills, sweetheart. Maybe I'll have you brought over early tomorrow. Now I want you to crouch down and suck my cock. Don't kneel. I don't want you to ruin your stockings. Not yet anyway."

Lana slid off of the fat man's lap and snuck in between his knees. He spread them wide for her and she had easy access to his long, thick cock. She circled it with her bright red lips and, with one hand on its base, pressed her head forwards, caressing it with her tongue. After all the cocksucking she had done while in training, she was overcome with embarrassment to be servicing this strange man's hardening pole dressed in her finery. It seemed sluttish, like she was doing some guy she had just met in the bathroom of a club back home. She was also afraid that one of the other girls might come in, a fear that was incongruous since all of them were sex slaves and subject to being ordered to perform similar acts at any time. What she did not know was that it was Danny's regular practice to get a blow job every night just before the girls went on. It relaxed him for the evening. So every one of the girls knew exactly what Lana was doing right now, even down to the position that she had assumed.

The slave girl's knees were spread wide to maintain her balance, and she could feel cool air running up her skirt, tickling her loins. Danny gave out a low moan as she forced the now hard cock deep into her mouth. Despite Danny's friendly attitude, she was afraid of him. He was a master, after all, and if he found fault with her, he could hurt her as much as any other.

Lana edged her body closer to the fat man as his cock began to pierce the edge of her throat. She placed her hand on his thigh for balance as she drew her head back and forth, giving the shaft the moist heat of her mouth. She ran her tongue over the cock's crown and tickled the tiny hole in the tip with the tip of her tongue. Danny placed his hands on her head lightly, not for purposes of control, but rather as a form of encouragement. His breath became heavy and his thighs began to shudder. "Ohhh, yes," he moaned. "Ohhhh, yeah."

The girl found herself getting excited in spite of herself. She snuck a hand under her skirt and gently caressed her moistening slit. She moaned faintly as she dragged her lips across the length of the club manager's hard meat. She felt the man stiffen. With a low moan, his cock began to pulse in her mouth. She could taste his salty discharge as it flooded her oral cavity. "Oh, fuck!" he yelled as his cock spasmed within her. "Oh, yeah! Suck it! Oh, yeah! Yeah!" he exclaimed.

When his orgasm subsided, Lana, after making sure she had consumed every drop of his sperm, let the softening meat slide from her mouth. Danny patted her on the head. "You're going to do all right, Lana."

Before he brought her upstairs he filled her in on some basic rules. Don't talk to the guests unless they talk to you. Let one of the more experienced girls take the lead. No alcohol unless the guest demanded it. Few of them would. Smile, be nice and make sure you clean yourself up after each use. "Most of the girls get two or three customers a night. You'll probably get more since you're new. Wash your cunt and ass good before you come back out of the room. And enjoy yourself. Dance up a storm. You're a beautiful, sexy, young woman, in the prime of your life. Make it happen. Okay?"

Lana nodded assent. Danny told her to use some mouth spray and then he'd take her upstairs. Each of the girls carried little purses to match their dresses and shoes. In it was breath spray, lotion, lubricant, lipstick, some tissues and a hairbrush.

After Lana had freshened her mouth and straightened her lipstick, Danny led her upstairs. Her pussy still tingled from her oral contact with Danny's stiff prick. She was slightly ashamed that she could get so excited sucking a stranger's cock. But as she walked up the stairs behind the heavyset man, she realized that all of her sexual skills would soon be out to the test and that it was probably a good thing that she could get into the proper spirit.

The girls were all waiting around, primping at the mirrored walls or talking quietly. Several had drinks of juice in front of them at the bar. At 8 o'clock sharp the music came on. Some of the girls started dancing with each other. Eventually some guests and a few supervisors wandered in.

The club was small enough so that it did not need a lot of people to feel comfortable. Lana watched as a man picked up one of the girls to dance. It was a meringue, and the girl started slowly, but after a minute, started to strut her stuff. By 8:30 there was a decent crowd. Lana had stood around anxiously. The beat of the music was somewhat comforting to her as it ran through. She found herself tapping her toe in time to the Latin beat. Finally, Yolanda came up to her and said, "There's someone I want you to meet."

Yolanda took Lana by the hand and guided her across the room. There were three men sitting at the bar, drinking and joking with one another. They were all in their late thirties and seemed to Lana to be fit and trim. A man with short black hair and olive colored skin got off of his chair and proffered it to Lana. Lana, discomfited by the fact of the man's deference to her, took the seat anyway. She was nervous. But the man was relaxed and teased her about her shyness. Yolanda had advised her to let the men talk and be pretty, and that's what she did. The man talked about his business, the golf game today, the weather. All the while, his eyes rested mostly on her proffered breasts. Lana decided to take matters in hand. "Would you like to dance?" she asked him.

The man, who had introduced himself as Vinnie, led her to the floor. It had become somewhat crowed and bodies were swirling and shaking all about them. The man took Lana's left hand in his and placed his other hand around her waist and they were off.

Slowly, Lana got into the spirit of the music's rhythm. The man was a confident and accomplished dancer and she soon found herself energized. He was handsome and that helped as Lana considered that he would probably want to go to one of the private rooms with her. His hips swung invitingly and his eyes were like blue stars.

After the first song, Vinnie wanted to stay on the dance floor and so they began again. Lana was in near heaven. Her body felt better than it had in weeks. She felt alive, free. Her hot red dress made her feel like a beauty queen. What were Cholo's words? Yes, a Latina princess. She smiled and laughed as the man and she danced song after song. Her body was sweaty with exertion, but as long as the man could keep up, she wanted to dance.

The club had been transformed from an empty room to a sea of whirling and turning excited people. Strobe lights flashed overhead and the lights on the floor flicked on and off in many different colors. The music was loud and almost deafening. But nobody wanted to talk. What had they really to talk about anyway? Everyone knew that the whole scene was just a charade. But no one cared. It was as if they had been transported to the hottest club in South Miami, or Brooklyn or East Los Angeles. This was not the music of your sophisticated uptown nightclub. It was Latino dance music and it mattered not a whit what the singers said, or the originality of the tune. The beat was all.

After their fifth dance together, Vinnie signaled that he wanted to return to the bar. Lana followed him, breathlessly. It had been wonderful, and her heart still beat hard in her chest. Her body felt exhilarated. Vinnie took a long pull of his martini and Lana sucked down a good portion of her juice. When he had replaced his glass on the bar, he looked at Lana with an appreciative gaze. She could tell that he was saying something to her, but she could not hear it over the music. She leaned her ear over to his mouth and she heard him yell into her ear, "Let's go upstairs."

Lana's heart almost stopped. It was the moment of truth. In a short while she would officially be a whore. Not by choice, but a whore nonetheless. The only difference was that her 'employer' was making all of the money. But from what she heard, whores back in the real world paid most of their money to their pimps anyway.

Lana swallowed hard and nodded, 'Yes' to her admirer. He took her hand and began to lead her to the stairs. They had to cut through the dance crowd and the jostling of the frantically moving bodies against hers made Lana aware of where they were going and what she would soon be doing.

When they broke free of the crowd, Vinnie led Lana up the steps. The upstairs consisted of a series of fifteen small rooms, each equipped with its own mini-bar, a large king sized bed and a whipping post. One for each slut on duty. The club's dancing staff consisted of twenty five girls. The ones not on duty in the club were generally either at rest back at the dormitory, or off on 'assignment' to a guest or supervisor. On nights that promised to be busy, more, or even all, the girls were added to the shift. There was no order of preference as to which whore used which room, and the patron was permitted to select any that were empty. They were all the same anyway.

The rooms ran around a gallery built up over the lower level. It surrounded the area covered by the dance floor and Lana could look down and see the writhing, dancing people as they walked along it. Vinnie selected the fourth room and opened the door and invited Lana inside.

The closing of the door muted the blasting music. It could still be heard, but it was now low enough to talk. The beat, however, the drumming beat of the percussion instruments, pulsed through the room like a throbbing heart.

Vinnie went to the bar and got himself another drink. Lana stood still, not sure what her next step should be. Vinnie turned to look at her and she returned his gaze. Vinnie was handsome and fit. Black hair peaked out from his robe by his chest. He had strong, but graceful hands. She could do worse, she thought.

Vinnie made the first move. He put down his drink and walked over to where Lana stood. He placed his strong hands on her shoulders and joined his lips to hers. Lana closed her eyes as she felt his hot tongue enter her mouth. Her loins began to tingle as Vinnie's tongue excited her. She placed her arms around his back and returned his kiss. She felt his hard body rub against hers.

Vinnie's hands gently grabbed the straps of her bodice and slowly worked them off of her shoulders. As the thin red straps worked their way down her arms, Lana lowered them, allowing the dress to be pulled down to her waist. Her ample, ripe breasts fell free.

Lana had been concerned as to how she would remove her dress. Would he order her to strip, like the slave she was? Or would it be up to her to initiate her nakedness for the man's lustful eyes? Either way, she would feel degraded and ashamed. But here this man had solved her problem. To show her breasts to him seemed the most natural thing in the world. His hands grasped them, delicately massaging them as his lips continued to inflame her. Her pussy tingled when he ran his thumbs across her stiff, hard nipples.

Now that her hands were liberated from her dress's straps, Lana used them to push open the sides of Vinnie's robe. She ran her hands over his strong chest, feeling the well developed muscles. Suddenly, the man tore off his robe. Lana took the opportunity to step out of her dress.

She began to lean over to take off her matching red shoes when Vinnie said, "Leave them on," undisguised passion in his voice.

They fell into the bed. Lana's cunt was wet and hot. Vinnie pushed her knees apart and poised his manhood at the entrance to her sheath. Taking her mouth again with his, he plunged his stiff rod inside.

Lana gasped when she felt her hot tunnel filled with Vinnie's hard cock. The man, overcome with passion and excitement, began to pump furiously. Lana, her mind befogged by lust responded, thrusting her hips up hard to meet his powerful strokes. She enveloped him with her arms, pulling his heat into her. Her stocking clad legs wrapped around his back, her bright red shoes dangling in the air, pushing his cock deeper inside her. When she felt him begin to come and felt his loud moan in her mouth, she came too, a jolt of electricity flowing through her body. She could feel his hot come splash against the walls of her womb. Her pussy gripped his piece hard with each powerful contraction. The beating of her heart seemed to match the tempo of music beneath them. When her contractions ebbed, she continued to grip his cock tightly with the newly developed muscles in her sheath. He groaned once more and then collapsed.

The pair made passionate love for the next hour. Lana took the initiative and drew Vinnie's cock to hardness with her mouth. For twenty minutes she made him moan and groan as she applied her oral skills to his aching rod. When she let him come, he yelled and shouted his pleasure. He took his turn at her loins, licking her engorged labia, running his hot tongue through the valley between them. He sucked on her clit until she squirmed and moaned in tortuous ecstasy. And then he plunged his hard meat into her, setting off an explosion of passion in her body. Afterwards, they lay entwined, like lovers do. He explored her curvaceous body with his hands, her breasts with his lips. She reached for his cock, but he stilled her hand with his. "Tomorrow," he whispered. He arose and crossed the dimly lit room to retrieve his robe. His cock hung flaccid between his legs. Before he left the room he gave her a long, lascivious look. "Thank you, Lana," he said and he left.

Lana rested for a few moments and then realized that someone would have the job of monitoring whether any of the girls were slacking off. She rose from the bed and washed herself in the bathroom, carefully rinsing her pussy in the bidet. She brushed her shoulder length black hair and freshened her makeup. When she had redonned her pretty, red dress, she exited the room to return to the bar. As soon as she opened the door, the intensity of the music struck her. She strutted down the gallery to the stairs, and turning at the top, looked at the frantically gyrating crowd below. She paused to take it in. Her hips seemed to adopt the beat of their own volition.

She remembered Cholo's insult to her. "No," she thought, "I am not a *crica*, a cunt, like Cholo called me. I am a red hot Latina *chica*." She walked down the steps slowly, her head up, swaying her hips to the beat, smiling.

CHAPTER ELEVEN
CODA

Sheila and Kit were assigned as waitresses in one of the restaurants. Sheila prospered. Her radiant good looks and matching smile garnered her the admiration of many a guest. It was rare that someone did not take her back to his room for the night. She became a favorite of several of the supervisors too. Her obvious enthusiasm for sucking cocks earned her many friends.

Kit, the proud little rich girl, however, was a different story. She was incompetent as a waitress. She was the recipient of many lashings for her failings. Although amused by her copious discharges, the staff soon grew tired of her ineptitude as a whore. After about a month, she was removed from the resort proper. She found herself and three other girls on the boat to the mainland. She was sold to an army brothel, where, after the officers had had their fill of her, she was assigned to service the enlisted men, averaging between twenty-five and thirty of them a day.

Mary had recovered from her injuries. She was the last of the aspiring models to be sent upstairs to the resort. Her experience with Huong had nearly broken her. She shivered in fear as her wrists were bound behind her and her gag installed. A tag was placed around her neck, denoting her destination.

As she was led naked and bound along the red brick pathways that late afternoon, the sky just beginning to darken, she began to cry. Her imagination ran wild with the vision of deliverance into the hands of some cruel master where she would be horribly and painfully mistreated.

She had no experience of the resort and had no idea where she was being led. She and her escort passed through the main resort area and climbed the hill to the supervisor's cottages. They passed several and then stopped at one which overlooked the steep cliffs on the western coast of the island. The guard knocked on the door. A brutish looking, well muscled man wearing the reddish brown robe of a supervisor answered the door. He thanked the guard, took hold of her leash, and led her inside. Mary's body shook as he removed her gag and unbound her wrists. Hoping to mollify any cruel intent he might have, she immediately assumed a kneeling position, her palms on her knees, her beautiful, round breasts proffered to the master. He looked down at her. "My name's Harry," he said.

The End